IN THE POCKET

Virginia Valley University

JESSICA RUDDICK

Peake Ink PRESS

Content edits provided by Marnee Blake.
Line editing suggestions provided by Red Adept Editing.

ISBN 978-1-946164-18-6

CHAPTER 1

Katie

I SWISHED MY straw around in my Coke, trying to keep my nostrils from flaring and failing miserably. It irked me when Danielle called me "Hollywood," which was of course why she did it. That, and she was already shit-faced. I couldn't fault her, though. She was the last of the four of us to turn twenty-one, and I *had* shown up late to her birthday bar crawl. She had the right to be a little peeved.

"Come on." Rachel nudged me off the stool. "We'll go get the next round."

Danielle raised her empty shooter glass in the air, her furry pink tiara tilting precariously on her head. "Get four shots for yourself, Hollywood! You're behind."

I ground my teeth, and Rachel tugged me away before I could say something I would regret. Though it wouldn't matter anyway—Danielle probably wouldn't remember most of the night. She was one of my best friends, but sometimes she could be an obnoxious drunk.

Closing my eyes for a moment, I checked my irritation and vowed to have a better attitude. Dani—and none of my other friends for that matter—didn't understand why the Hollywood nickname bothered me so much. They didn't understand how close to the mark it hit, how it poured salt in an open wound, especially when I was being taunted by a voicemail from my sister that I hadn't yet listened to.

"Why were you late anyway?" Rachel asked. We'd been randomly paired up as roommates freshman year, and she'd been my bestie ever since. Danielle and her best friend, Destiny, had lived across the hall from us. Now in our junior year, they shared the apartment next door to mine and Rachel's.

"I was meeting with Dr. Jenkins."

Rachel scrunched up her perfectly freckled nose. Her hair was auburn—*and don't you dare call it red*—and she had the fair skin to match. "At nearly ten at night?"

"I caught him after his evening class ended at nine."

"And it couldn't wait until morning?"

It could have, but I would have stewed about the comments he'd made on my paper all night. I was a biology major with a premed concentration, and I'd taken his Shakespeare class for fun. I'd be damned if I got anything less than an A.

I shrugged and tried to flag down the bartender. When she ignored me, I sighed. "I can't believe how busy this place is. It's *Tuesday*."

It was Rachel's turn to shrug. Though she was a good student, she wasn't as fastidious about her grades as I was. I could count on one hand the number of times I'd been out past eleven on a school night.

We finally returned to our table with four shooters, but two guys I didn't recognize had taken our seats. Danielle and Destiny were flirting mercilessly with them, but as soon as Destiny saw us approach, she shooed them away like pesky gnats.

"They could have stayed," I said.

Danielle shook her head, her silky blond hair swaying with the movement. "No way. I want to spend my twenty-first with my *giiiirrrrrllllsssss!*" She wrapped her hand around my neck and pulled my face closer so she could plant a big, wet kiss on my cheek. She grabbed the shooter I'd placed in front of her, and half of the bright liquid sloshed out onto the table as she raised it. "To my *giiiirrrrlllllssss!*"

"To Danielle on her twenty-first birthday!" Rachel corrected. "May you not worship the porcelain gods tonight."

Laughing, Destiny eyed her best friend. "Unlikely."

"Truth." Glassy-eyed, Danielle grinned then abruptly became teary eyed. "I love you girls. You know that, right?"

Destiny pulled her into a hug. Danielle had a big heart that bruised easily, and I wanted to bitch-slap myself for being late tonight of all nights. I should have swallowed my obsession with my grades for one evening and not disappointed my friend on her birthday.

I immediately forgave her for calling me "Hollywood" earlier. It was such a stupid thing anyway. She thought my penchant for wearing oversized designer sunglasses made me look like a celebrity hiding from paparazzi. I would never tell her why the seemingly innocent nickname grated on me so much, which only piqued her curiosity. As a rule, she only used it when she was drunk or irritated with me. Tonight met both of those criteria.

"I'm getting the next round!" I declared, preparing to fight my way back to the bar again.

"You got the last one," Destiny protested. "I'll get it."

I shook my head. "Nope. I was late. Consider it my penance."

As I weaved through the mass of people, my phone vibrated in my back pocket. *Damn it.* No doubt it was Kassidy calling again, but I didn't want to deal with her drama tonight. Hell, I never wanted to deal with it, but such was my life.

I let the call go to voicemail again. I would deal with her tomorrow.

* * *

I WAS SHIT-FACED. Ultimately and utterly shit-faced.

Giggling, I stumbled down the sidewalk, my arm looped with Danielle's. "Make way for the birthday princess!" I announced. No one paid me any attention. Although I felt like my obnoxious level was dialed up to eleven, my antics were tame. Our sleepy little college town had seen much crazier.

Somewhere deep in my brain, warning bells were screaming. I made it a rule to fly under the radar, and I was breaking that rule. *Tomorrow. I'll worry about it tomorrow, along with my stupid Shakespeare paper and Kassidy.*

Kassidy... I was always worrying about Kassidy. *Nope, not tonight.*

I giggled again, and behind me, Rachel snorted. Once she'd seen my alcohol consumption go up, hers had taken a nosedive.

Glancing over my shoulder at her, I grinned. "You're the best roomie ever!"

She grabbed my arm, preventing me from taking a tumble off the curb. "Watch your step, Giggle Girl."

For some reason, I found that hilarious. That nickname was *loads* better than Hollywood.

"Here we are!" Destiny pointed at a rickety wooden staircase that led to an establishment aptly named Top of the Stairs. While sober, I'd wondered who had thought it was a good idea to force inebriated college students to tackle the steep stairs. But tonight, I welcomed the challenge.

Unfortunately for me, my excitement came to a standstill as I noticed the line starting at the bouncer and trailing down the steps. I groaned but didn't complain. We'd promised Danielle a proper bar crawl, which meant at least one drink at each of the bars downtown.

When we finally gained admission, I realized with one glance why it was so crowded—several key players from the football team were holding court in the corner of the room.

I watched as Wyatt Archer, quarterback extraordinaire, raised a solitary finger. Within seconds, a server placed a new bottle in his hand. He took a swig without missing a beat in his conversation with his number one wide receiver, Freddie Martin, better known as FM4. Both of them were either oblivious to the girls vying for their attention, or the guys were ignoring them. *Interesting.* Snarky thoughts flooded my mind, but I pushed them away. I couldn't care less about the local football gods, so I wasn't going to waste my brain power.

"Ooh," Danielle squealed. "This just got better. Do you think if I tell them it's my birthday, they'll buy me a drink?"

Laughing, Destiny shook her head. "Oh no, honey. That's not how that works. You'll be lucky if the Archer and FM4 let *you* buy *them* a drink."

Danielle stuck her lip out in a pout, but it was short lived. "To the bar!" She pointed ahead.

The Archer. That was what they called Wyatt Archer because one, that was his name, and two, like the legendary archer Robin Hood, he never missed his mark.

Well, not *never*, but his passing record was pretty darn good. He'd started breaking school records his freshman year and hadn't let up since. I was enough of a football fan to appreciate that. But I had enough self-esteem to steer clear of him. Wyatt Archer had enough girls throwing themselves at him. Case in point, the curvy redhead putting her hand on his arm, flipping her hair over her shoulder, and leaning in such a way to offer him a clear view of her ample cleavage.

No, thank you.

"Why are you staring at him?" Rachel whispered in my ear, causing me to jump.

"I'm not." Except I totally was, which was why her comment had caught me by surprise because I didn't care. *I didn't.* But it was too late—Wyatt appeared to have noticed me. My first instinct was to look behind me to see if I was mistaken, because why would he be looking at me? Sure, I was attractive, but there were much flashier girls in the room. But then his blue eyes locked onto mine, and his mouth twisted into a smirk. *Yup, he's definitely looking at me.* He raised his beer bottle in a cheers fashion before bringing it to his perfect lips.

His perfect lips? What the hell, Katie? Get your shit together.

I could feel my cheeks flushing, so I dragged Rachel with me to catch up with Danielle and Destiny. Destiny placed a drink in my hand. I had no idea what it was because I'd never been a big drinker, but it wasn't a shot or a shooter, and for that, I was grateful. The trek up the stairs had given my brain enough time to come to the conclusion that I needed to slow down.

Five minutes and half of that evil drink later, I wondered why I'd considered cutting myself off. It was Danielle's twenty-first birthday, and she'd only have one. What kind of friend would I be if I left her high and dry?

Destiny put her finger over the end of her straw then brought it up to her mouth and released the liquid. "Good God, Katie, stop staring."

I whipped my head around. "I'm not."

I totally was. Damn it.

Danielle grinned. "I wouldn't have thought you'd be attracted to a dumb jock."

"He's not dumb," I said automatically. Three sets of eyebrows simultaneously rose, and my cheeks flushed again. "I had a class with him last year," I muttered. "He's actually pretty smart."

Danielle and Destiny's eyes widened. "What?" Danielle squealed. "You never told us that."

I flipped my hair over my shoulder, going for nonchalant. "Because it wasn't a big deal. We sat in the same classroom three hours a week. It's not like we became friends or anything. He probably doesn't even know my name."

Rachel chuckled. "Methinks the lady doth protest too much."

That should have been my line. I was the one who had been late to the bar crawl because I was meeting with my Shakespeare professor.

I flipped my hair over my other shoulder. "Whatever." That was pretty lame as far as comebacks went, but it was the best my compromised brain could come up with.

"You should go say hi," Destiny suggested.

I snorted. "No."

She shrugged. "Suit yourself."

While I could appreciate how cute the cowlick in Wyatt's hair was, that was no reason for me to talk to him. Other than his buddy FM4, he was the most famous student on our campus. Hell, he was one of the most famous college students in the country. And that was *exactly* why he was the last person I should concern myself with.

I got more than my fill of high-profile drama from Kassidy. I could only imagine what it would be like to date the Archer.

Date him? What the hell, Katie? Destiny was only talking about saying hi to him, not dating him. Anyway, it didn't matter because both of those options were ridiculous.

I nodded, having thoroughly talked myself out of humiliating myself. The pang of doubt took me by surprise. I'd never been one to seek the spotlight—I was more comfortable in the shadows—but something about Wyatt Archer made me want to be in his spotlight.

Where the hell did that thought come from? If I hadn't already known I'd had too much to drink, that would have clinched it. Yet the thought wasn't so easily erased from my mind. I lowered my mouth to the straw in my drink, thinking that if the drink had giveth that thought, then the drink could also taketh away.

CHAPTER 2

Wyatt

I STRETCHED, TRYING to ease the tightness in my traps. Half a second later, a beer bottle appeared in my outstretched hand. *Damn.* That wasn't what I'd intended, but I wasn't going to turn away a cold drink. As I took a swig, I tried to ignore the redhead who'd sidled up to me twenty minutes ago and hadn't taken the hint. There were some perks of being the university's quarterback that never got old. And others? Let's just say they'd lost their appeal.

Truth be told, I wasn't in the mood to be out that night, but my number one receiver, Freddie—known to the media as FM4—was celebrating. He'd just declared his eligibility for the draft.

He clanked his bottle against mine in a toast of sorts. "It's not too late, man. You could still declare."

I tilted the bottle back, nearly draining it. We'd had this conversation too many times to count, but FM4 was relentless on and off the field.

"Nah, not this year." I didn't bother to explain my reasoning for the umpteenth time. The logic would be lost on my friend in his inebriated state. Hell, it was lost on him when he wasn't drunk. Besides that, I wasn't going to get into it with so many hangers-on around.

He shook his head. "You're missing out. You'd go first round."

I shrugged. He was right, and it was tempting as hell.

"Who you gonna pass to next year?" He spread his arms wide. "Half of the magic is leaving."

Another truth. The two of us had broken the school record for most completed passes in a season, and so far, Coach Gurgin hadn't impressed me with his roster of new recruits. *Damn.* Any quarterback worth his salt knew perfect passes didn't mean shit unless there was someone on the other end to catch them.

I momentarily scowled but quickly wiped the look off my face. Freddie had made the best decision for him. I respected that and wouldn't ruin his celebration. It wasn't his fault his plans didn't align with mine.

"Half? Really?" I grinned. "More like thirty percent. *Maybe* forty."

"Pssshhh." But Freddie grinned back at me.

Damn. I was going to miss his ugly mug.

Maybe he was right. Maybe I should throw my lot in with his. I'd already won the Heisman and a national championship. What did I have to stick around for?

As the question entered my head, I could hear my dad's voice as clearly as if he were sitting right next to me: *Don't take anything for granted, son. One bad hit, and your career is over.*

That had happened to him. He'd entered the draft his junior year and gone seventh, securing a position with Cleveland. Then the third game of the season, Dad had gotten blindsided by the defense in what should have been a routine handoff. It had been a personal foul, but that fifteen-yard penalty hadn't fixed my dad's back. Neither had three surgeries. Cleveland had dropped him at the end of the season.

My mother had dropped him, too, but that was another story.

Shitty luck, he'd always said. Even shittier was how freely the docs had given him pain meds. It had taken him years to kick the addiction. By then, he was a nobody, not even a has-been—he was a could-have-been. He had no degree, and the money he'd gotten for his one year on the roster was gone.

Of course, I'd been too young to realize what the hell was going on. I'd lived with my grandparents then, and they'd kept me blissfully unaware. But I sure as hell was aware now. It was hard not to be when reporters threw that family history in my face every few months. I got it— it was a social-interest piece. But it was also my life.

"Aww, come on, man." Freddie nudged my shoulder. "You're depressing me."

I neutralized my expression. "Sorry."

"You know what would cheer you up?" Freddie grinned. "An eight-figure salary, just for throwing a few balls."

I gripped my beer bottle tighter. "You test the waters first and tell me how it is."

The redhead scooted over. If she got any closer, she would be sitting in my lap. Her perfume was so pungent, my eyes burned. I didn't even know the chick. Hell, she didn't know me, not really. I was the Archer, and that was all she was interested in.

Stretching my arm out and wrapping it around her, I eased into the role of the quarterback playboy. Only somehow, it didn't fit as well as it used to.

Beside me, the girl beamed and pressed her tits against my side, making sure I felt them. *No worries, honey.* A guy would've had to be impotent not to notice.

"My name is Brittany," she said breathily into my ear. "I'm ready to leave when you are."

Two years ago, I would have taken her up on the offer immediately. Last year, I would have given it another hour to be a tease. But now her words only made me tired.

* * *

Katie

DESTINY SHOVED ME forward. I didn't have to see her face to know she was smirking. Inhaling deeply, I put one foot in front of the other then spun around.

"We've been here an hour," I said. "This bar crawl has come to a stop. We should move on."

Rolling her eyes, Destiny spun me and whispered in my ear. "Chicken." Then she shoved me again.

The childish taunt was stupid, but it was enough to move me forward. A few seconds of embarrassment, and then I would be on my way. *No problem.*

But the closer I got to Wyatt Archer, the more my gut churned. I wasn't a puker, but the contents of my stomach were dangerously sloshing around. As if asking out the Archer in the middle of TOTS wouldn't bring me enough unwanted attention. Spewing at his feet would make me infamous.

With each step, I tried to come up with a reasonable excuse to bail, but my brain wasn't working correctly. *Obviously.* Or I wouldn't have gotten sucked in by Destiny's dare.

I cast a final glance over my shoulder to find my three friends intently watching. The only thing that was missing was the popcorn.

Screw this. If they wanted a show, I would give them a show.

The redhead who was sitting next to Wyatt gave me a nasty look, and I gave her one right back. I jerked my head. "Beat it."

Her jaw dropped. "Are you serious?"

Though my gaze was focused on the girl, Wyatt caught my attention as his eyebrows shot up. A grin stretched across his face, and I could imagine what he was thinking.

Girl fight. It probably wouldn't be the first time girls had fought over him. Too bad it wasn't happening. I didn't know the other girl, but I could read her well enough to know she wasn't a fighter. Neither was I, but she didn't know that.

I narrowed my eyes at her. "Get lost."

She looked at Wyatt to save her. He merely shrugged. *Yup. Read that right too.* For whatever reason, he had no interest in that girl. Perhaps redheads weren't his flavor of choice this week. *Let's hope he likes brunettes.*

Fuming, the girl stomped off. The tiny part of me that was still sober felt bad—I normally wasn't a bitch. But I was doing her a favor. Did she really want to be next in the line of the Archer's conquests? I conveniently ignored the logic that at the moment, I was no better than her.

Except, yes, I was. I had enough dignity to make him buy me dinner first. I wasn't planning to go home with him straight from the bar like that girl was.

I ran my hands over my hips and positioned my lips into a pout, which was a signature Kassidy move. *Don't think about that.* "Is this seat taken?"

Beside Wyatt, FM4 laughed. "No, honey, it isn't. Not anymore. You cleared it out."

His comment annoyed me, so I cocked my head at him. "Where's Angela tonight?"

The smile dropped off his face, and he pulled his arms in and away from the girls sitting next to him. "She's, uh, she's sick."

He is so whipped. It was kind of cute, actually. I'd never met Angela, but his girlfriend, who'd been his high school sweetheart, had a reputation for not taking any shit.

I focused my attention back on Wyatt and ran my tongue over my lips, which was probably overkill, but I wasn't going for an Academy Award. I was only looking to prove to my friends that I wasn't a lame stick-in-the-mud. "Can I sit?"

Wyatt nodded, his blue eyes studying me. I slid into place next to him. *Damn, he smells good.* Though I'd had a class with him, I'd never been this close to him before. His chiseled jawline had a thin coating of stubble, but since it was blond, like his hair, it wasn't noticeable. *That must be convenient.* My hair was dark, and I got a five o'clock shadow on my legs that was annoying as hell.

I could picture Kassidy wrinkling her nose and running a perfectly manicured hand down her smooth leg. *I can't believe you haven't done laser hair removal yet*, she would say.

He turned his face toward me, and I saw that his blue eyes had flecks of gold near the pupils. They continued to study me, and in that instant, I realized he wasn't drunk. Not by a long shot. Somehow knowing that he was sober while I was wasted made the situation even more uncomfortable.

It's only a performance. Yeah, but I'd left that behind years ago.

The edges of his mouth quirked up, and my confidence faltered. *Why didn't I bring my drink with me?*

"I'm Katelyn Sullivan." I cringed. This wasn't roll call— he didn't need my full name. I cleared my throat and tried again. "Katie. I go by Katie."

Not much better. I wanted to look over at my friends, but I couldn't bear it if they were laughing. I never should have gotten sucked in by their dare. Just as I was about to throw in the towel and slink away, Wyatt spoke.

"I know who you are."

* * *

Wyatt

"You do?" Katie's voice came out in a squeak.

"Yeah. You were in my philosophy class." I normally kept to myself in class, but that one had been discussion based, which had forced me to interact. Whenever I'd spoken, everyone else in class would bob their heads up and down like they were plastic figurines on a dashboard, but not this girl. She was the only one who'd challenged me, calling me out on some shit I had said and raking my ass over the coals. I didn't even remember what we'd been discussing, but I remembered the feeling. It was one of the few times in my life that I'd ever been embarrassed. It had been kind of refreshing.

So yeah, I would have remembered her even if she hadn't possessed a kind of an old-world beauty. Her hair was long and dark, and it had always been pulled away from her face. She'd never worn makeup, not that she needed it. She was classically beautiful, like a movie star from the black-and-white movies my grandmother had been fond of.

Even now, her hair was pulled into an unassuming ponytail, and her face was clear, except for a little something at her eyes. Mascara... yeah, that was it. She wasn't trying to compete with the other girls in the bar, but she didn't have to because she'd beaten them hands down anyway. The others might be hot, but she was beautiful.

"Oh," Katie said, seeming flustered. "I didn't think you'd remember me."

Maybe she'd forgotten our heated debates. She was smart—that much had been clear. She probably handed her classmates their asses all the time. Maybe I was an arrogant prick for figuring she would remember the time she'd handed me mine, just because I was the Archer.

"How could I forget the girl who made me feel this big?" I held up two fingers an inch apart.

Her cheeks turned bright pink, and her eyes shifted to the ground. I should have felt like an ass for making her feel bad, but I was too busy enjoying looking at her. The girl intrigued me, and not many did.

She moved her gaze up, focusing on something across the crowded bar. No, not something—*someone.* Multiple someones. Three chicks gaped at her, and I assumed they were her friends.

She ran her hands over the thighs of her pants, and a fierce determination gleamed in her eyes. She tilted her head, giving me a clear view of the smooth skin on her neck. Her full, unpainted lips parted a little, fixing into a pout.

My jeans suddenly felt tighter. I couldn't figure her out—she definitely knew what she was doing, but it was like she didn't realize how good at it she was. Normally, chicks overestimated their sexual appeal. Katie did the opposite. *Jesus.* It was a good thing this girl didn't know how dangerous she was.

"Sorry about that," she said, only she didn't sound sorry.

I couldn't help it. I laughed. "No, you're not."

Her eyes widened, and I realized they were more hazel than brown. She was wearing all black, and I wondered if her eyes would look green if she wore that color.

It took her a beat to collect herself. "Well, will you forgive me anyway?"

Shrugging, I reached for my beer bottle. "Sure." When I put it down, I realized she didn't have a drink. "Do you want something?" I gave a wave, and a barmaid appeared almost immediately. "What do you want?" I asked Katie.

She shook her head. "I'm good."

"Not even water or a soda?" I asked. "Come on. It's on my tab."

Katie shook her head again.

The barmaid smiled, her eyes narrowing as she looked at Katie. It was obvious she didn't mind being at my beck and call, but she was annoyed to wait for Katie, which annoyed me.

I looked over at Katie's friends, who immediately averted their gazes. *How smooth, ladies.* They'd obviously been staring at us. I pointed. "She'll have one of those red things that they're having. And a water."

When the barmaid walked away, Katie quietly said, "You didn't have to do that."

"Yeah, I did." I took a swig from my bottle. Normally, chicks fell all over themselves with gratitude if I bought them a drink, which I rarely did anymore. There was no point—the end result was the same either way. And while I stood to make a shit ton of money one day, I wasn't there yet. My scholarship only went so far, and my dad didn't have a lot of extra money to send me. But for some reason, my answer was true—I needed to get her a drink. It didn't make any sense.

"If you really want to buy someone a drink, it would make my friend's night if you bought her one. It's her birthday."

I looked over at the trio of girls and noticed for the first time that one was wearing a plastic tiara lined with pink fur.

"Sure," I said smoothly. I raised my beer bottle and nodded in her direction. The three of them squealed.

Christ. I needed to get home. I really wasn't in the right frame of mind for this. Case in point? I was reading way too much into the current situation with Katie. She was probably like every other chick who was hoping for fifteen minutes of fame by being with me. Or worse, she was hoping to latch on to me before I hit it big. Freddie was lucky to have Angela. They'd been together forever, so he'd never had to worry whether she was using him.

The barmaid returned with Katie's drink, and while I ordered one for the birthday girl, Katie downed half of it. *So much for not needing a drink.*

When I looked down at her, her lips were tinged red from whatever the hell was in that drink. *Aw, hell.* I wanted to suck it off and see what it tasted like, see what *she* tasted like.

I tore my gaze away from her mouth and looked at Freddie, who was talking with a few of the guys who'd finally shown up. *Good.* I would be able to leave soon.

"So, do you want to go out sometime?" Katie asked in a rush, bringing my attention back to her.

"Excuse me?" Those were not words I'd expected to come out of her mouth. When was the last time a nice girl had asked me out? I couldn't remember. The answer might be never. I couldn't blame them, though. I'd made my bed when I'd developed a reputation as a player. But hell, if a girl wanted to use me, then I had no problem using her right back. Or at least I used to.

Katie looked away as more words tumbled out of her mouth. "Dinner. A date. You and me." She finished off her drink, still avoiding my gaze.

I didn't respond, wanting her to look at me before answering. It was so weird—she vacillated between boldness and shyness, but both seemed to fit her. I couldn't figure her out.

Finally, her eyes met mine, and I brought my face close to hers. She inhaled sharply and waited for me to speak.

"Yes."

CHAPTER 3

Katie

I LIFTED MY head and groaned. *Why the hell am I wearing a brick helmet? And why does my mouth taste like a litter box?*

As if she could read my mind, Rachel's cat, Princess Buttercup, fluffed her tail in my face, jumped off the bed, and sauntered off. "Sorry," I croaked, feeling stupidly guilty for silently insulting the cat, "but your litter box stinks." When Rachel had returned to the apartment after summer break, she'd brought the cat with her. I was more of a dog person, but for some reason, the tabby had taken a liking to me. I didn't pretend to understand it.

I blindly reached for the alarm clock, and as the red numbers came into focus, I jumped out of bed. *Shit! It was 10:17!* I had a nine o'clock class. Wincing as the pounding in my head beat me into submission, I sagged back onto the bed. I'd already missed the entire class, and my next one wasn't until one, so there was no point working myself into a tizzy.

Rachel showed up in my bedroom doorway with a smile on her face and a bowl of cereal in her hand. "Good morning, sunshine!" Princess Buttercup laced herself between my roommate's legs.

"I overslept," I grumbled. "My alarm wasn't on."

She shook her head. "Why don't you use your cell phone's alarm like the rest of the modern world? Then you wouldn't have to remember to turn it on every night. And then maybe I wouldn't hear it through the walls at oh-dark-thirty."

"That was *one* time," I protested. "And it wasn't my fault. Princess Butterbutt sat on the volume button."

Rachel looked down and made kissing noises at the cat. "Not my princess."

I rolled my eyes and immediately regretted it when the throbbing in my forehead responded to the eye movement. Thank God the four of us were all twenty-one now. No more birthday bar crawls for me.

"How are the Double Ds?" I asked. Dani and Destiny had given themselves that nickname freshman year, and it had stuck.

"I haven't heard from either of them yet this morning." Rachel wagged her eyebrows suggestively. "Speaking of hearing from people, have you heard from the Archer today?"

I frowned. "Why would I..." I trailed off as parts of the prior evening came into focus. *Drinking too many fruity drinks, throwing myself at Wyatt, having even more fruity drinks, exuberantly announcing to Main Street that I was dating the Archer.* "Oh God."

Rachel grinned as she chomped on her Cheerios. "Is it all coming back to you now?"

I held my face in my hands. "How could you let me do that?"

"Which part?"

"All of it. Every last little bit." If being hung over hadn't already made me feel sick to my stomach, the mortification would have.

My roommate shrugged. "It was nice to see you cut loose for once." The next three words went unspoken— *you're too uptight.* She grinned. "And if you get a little *bow chicka wow wow* out of the Archer as a result, then so be it."

"That's sooo not going to happen."

"Why not?" Her grin widened. "I hear he's a sure thing."

"*Oh... my... God.*" I stared at her, but she had no shame and continued leering at me with her toothy grin. "It's not going to happen because one—I'm not that kind of girl." Rachel rolled her eyes. "And two—I'm not actually going on a date with him."

"Yes, you are. This Friday at seven o'clock. You made all of us put it in our phones."

"No, I didn't." Except some of what she was saying sounded vaguely familiar.

"Hang on." Rachel ducked out of the room, and when she returned, she was holding her phone instead of the cereal bowl. "Here." She held it out for me to see—*Katie's date with the Golden God.*

"The Golden God? Seriously?"

"Your words, not mine."

I flopped onto my bed and threw my arm over my eyes. "I'm never drinking again."

* * *

Wyatt

MY MUSCLES SCREAMED as I pushed the bar off my chest. Except they weren't screaming in agony. No, they were yelling an enthusiastic *hell yes!* Nothing beat the burn of feeling my body getting stronger.

That was a lie. Scoring the game-winning touchdown beat it hands down. But one wouldn't be possible without the other.

"Fuck yeah." Freddie guided the bar onto the rack.

I exhaled. "Add five on each side."

"What?" Clucking his tongue, Freddie shook his head. "Nah, man. You're maxed out."

He was probably right, but we wouldn't know for sure until I tried. "The hell I am."

Something on the other side of the gym caught Freddie's attention. *Not surprising.* Ever since he'd declared for the draft and signed with an agent, he'd had trouble focusing. I got it—his entire life was about to change, so he had every right to be on edge. That was one of the reasons we were in the gym in the first place. While his performance over the past three seasons spoke for itself, he still had the combines to contend with and wanted to be ready.

I sat up and looked over. The TV was tuned to ESPN, but the volume was muted.

"Hang on." Freddie trotted over to the TV, where *College Football Roundup* was showing. He turned the sound up.

"Jacksonville needs a wide receiver. Heck, if we're being honest here, Jacksonville needs a little bit of everything. They've got two first-round picks." Howie Umbert turned to his co-commentator, Phil Manchester. *"What are you thinking?"*

Phil straightened the stack of papers in front of him. *"Lance Zigler out of Ohio is an obvious choice. But they also couldn't go wrong with FM4."*

"FM4 is no good to them unless they get a passing quarterback," Howie shot back. *"You know that."*

"Jacksonville," Freddie muttered. "I don't know if I want to end up there."

"Don't worry," I told him. "Bob is the best. He'll take care of you." Bob Harridan was the older-than-dirt legendary sports agent Freddie had signed with. Bob only took a handful of new clients each season, so Freddie had gotten lucky.

"While we're on the subject of FM4," Phil said, *"I'm going to address the elephant in the room. Wyatt Archer is*

making a mistake. How can he not enter the draft after a national championship? Why stick around? What else does he hope to accomplish?"

Freddie reached for the controls again. For a second, I considered telling him to leave it, but I let him turn it off.

"Sorry, man." Freddie clapped me on the shoulder. "That guy is a dick."

"It's cool." I'd learned long ago to ignore the media. Usually, I did that by not tuning in at all, but sometimes, it snuck in. The trick was not letting other people's talk get into my head.

Too bad I was failing at that. I wasn't an idiot—I knew what people were saying. But knowing it was a lot different than hearing it on a national sports show.

Freddie cocked his head. "You okay?"

I scrubbed a hand over my face and sank back onto the bench. "Am I making a mistake?"

My buddy's expression told me he didn't want to answer the question.

"Seriously, Freddie. Am I fucking up?"

Freddie sighed. "Nobody knows what's best for you except you. You want to stick around here for another year?" He spread his arms wide, gesturing to the state-of-the-art gym we were in. "That don't work for me. Hell, lasting four years was never going to work for me. But you've got brains in that thick skull of yours."

Freddie, like a lot of the other guys, had taken the bare minimum course load to keep his eligibility. Along with that came bare minimum effort, which meant his grades barely made the cut. I didn't like to get up in his business, so I didn't know for sure, but I suspected he was close to flunking out.

"You're not stupid, Freddie."

"I never said I was. I'm just not interested. That's all. Getting a degree was never part of my plan."

"Yeah." To Freddie, college was the minor leagues and nothing else. He saw the education part as nothing more than a necessary inconvenience.

Freddie shrugged. "Hell, maybe I'm the one who's fucking up. Maybe I'm not ready for the big time."

I snorted. "Yeah, right." Freddie was more than ready. If he could have gone after freshman year, he would have.

"I know." He grinned. "I'm gonna tear that shit up. I was trying on that modesty thing for size."

I laughed. Trying to fit modesty into Freddie's ego was like trying to squeeze a Mack truck through a doorway. Many called FM4 cocky, but to play at our level, players had to have confidence that bordered on cockiness. The difference between Freddie and me was that I didn't flash mine around.

I knew I was the best college quarterback in the country. It wasn't being cocky if it was a simple fact. But I also knew my gut was telling me that I wasn't ready to go pro. So far, my gut had never steered me wrong—at least not when it came to the important stuff—and I hated that the media hype was making me question it.

* * *

Katie

MY HAND SHOOK as I rubbed moisturizer onto my cheeks. Breaking off my date with Wyatt was necessary— inevitable, even—but for some reason, I hesitated to make the call.

Because it's awkward.

Yeah, that was all it was—I wanted to avoid the awkward conversation. I could text him, but I thought he deserved a phone call rather than a text.

Yeah, right. My backing out of our date would barely register on his radar. He was the Archer—he had girls throwing themselves at him every day. I was nothing special to him. Breaking our plans by text instead of a call would be quicker and easier for both of us.

I shook off the feeling that maybe I was putting it off because deep down, I didn't want to cancel. Maybe I wanted to see our date through, to feel Wyatt's intense gaze travel up and down my body.

Ridiculous. I grabbed my phone and quickly pounded out a text. *Have to cancel our date. Sorry!*

I hit send before I had time to obsess about it further. Satisfied, I placed the phone on the dresser so I could focus on getting ready.

Seconds later, the phone rang. My eyes bugged out when I saw the caller's name. It was him. He was calling me. *What the hell?* I should let it go to voice mail. I shouldn't answer it.

My hand suddenly became possessed and not connected to my brain. It was like it acted of its own fruition to pick up the phone and tap the button to accept the call.

Wincing, I put the phone up to my ear. "Hello?"

"You want to reschedule?" His deep voice flooded my auditory senses. No greeting, no preamble—he got straight to business.

"Um..." I stalled for time. This wasn't part of the plan. He was supposed to see my text, shrug, and move on with his life. He wasn't supposed to call me and actually act interested.

"Katie?"

I closed my eyes. "Yes, I'm still here."

"When are you free?"

"I'm free Friday," I blurted out. "I mean seven o'clock doesn't work for me, but I could do a little later. Maybe seven thirty."

A long pause filled the line, and I put my hand over my eyes, completely mortified and thankful he couldn't see me. Now it would be his turn to completely call off the date. No way would he want to go out with a blubbering moron.

"Sure," he said. "I can do that."

Relief flooded me, and I took my hand off my eyes. "Great. So I'll see you Friday." I tried to keep the eagerness out of my voice.

"Looking forward to it."

He is? What the hell?

"Okay, bye!" I hurriedly disconnected and flung the phone onto the bed. *What just happened?* That was one of the weirdest phone calls I'd ever had, and with Kassidy's tendencies to drunk dial me, that was saying something.

This is a mistake. I should have stood firm. I shouldn't have let the deep timbre of his voice turn me to mush. But there was no way I could cancel a second time. My pride and dignity couldn't withstand it.

At least the date would only take a few hours of my time. It wouldn't take long for him to realize that I wasn't his type. I was overly serious and boring, which was how I'd gotten myself into this mess in the first place. I never should have risen to Destiny's bait. I *liked* boring. It was stable with no drama.

So I would waste a few hours of my and Wyatt's time on Friday night then wash my hands of this silliness. I nodded, feeling better about the situation. Then I looked at the clock and cursed. *Damn it.* If I didn't get my ass in gear, I was going to be late to my afternoon classes. I hurriedly finished getting ready. Only when I tucked my phone into my backpack did I remember that I'd never listened to Kassidy's voice mail. I calculated how long I could feasibly ignore it and use the excuse that I hadn't noticed it. *Not much longer.*

I sighed. A voice mail from Kassidy was never good—it meant she wanted something. If it were something simple, she would have texted. Vowing to deal with her that evening, I rushed out the door to my one o'clock class.

* * *

Wyatt

I STARED DOWN at the blinking text on my phone from Katelyn Sullivan. Though she went by Katie, when she'd entered her information into my phone the previous night, she'd typed in her full name.

That had been one awkward phone call. I didn't know what had possessed me to call her back like that. I was the Archer. I didn't need to chase chicks.

Maybe that was why Katie intrigued me. I'd had girls play hard to get before, but what they were doing had been obvious. That didn't seem to be the case with Katie. She legitimately didn't want to be gotten.

Which of course made me want her. *How fucked up is that?*

The facade she'd presented last night was just that—a facade. It was a fake, made-up version of herself. Even if I hadn't remembered her from class, I would still know because I'd spent years learning to read people. It was one of the things that made me a good quarterback. Katie had been uncomfortable in her own skin, almost like she'd been trying on someone else's. *But whose?*

Hell if I knew. And I didn't know why I cared. I had more important things to think about.

I strode out of the locker room and squinted as the sun glinted off the fresh layer of snow. I could catch a shuttle that would take me to the academic side of campus, but I preferred to walk. Most people were so bundled up against the cold and focused on getting to their destination that they didn't notice me. Walking through campus in winter was a much different experience than in warmer months.

I checked the time and picked up my pace to a jog. *Damn.* I envied Freddie, who'd stayed behind at the gym. For the most part, I enjoyed my classes, but I was heading to a lower-level geology class I was taking to satisfy a core requirement. Most students took these sorts of classes their freshman year. My schedule was tricky, though, because of the demands of football, so it hadn't fit in until now. Not only was it a class about freaking rocks, but I stuck out like... well, a junior quarterback in a mix of scrawny freshmen. Worse, the professor had pointed me out on the first day of class, so I felt like I had to set an example for these kids—I couldn't skip class, even though I could probably pass by only reading the lecture notes.

So much more shit was involved in playing football than just playing football. The high-profile players' actions were scrutinized on and off the field. I'd never been naive enough to think there would never be negative press about my performance, but I hadn't realized how quickly the rest of my life would be perpetually under the microscope. I thought I would at least have until I went pro before I had to worry about shit like this. And even then, some pro players managed to keep their home lives private.

I'd brought some of this shit on myself—I'd been young, reckless, and stupid my first year and a half. It wasn't until the middle of my sophomore season that I'd stopped fucking around and focused on what really mattered—playing ball. It had always been playing ball.

I fucking loved it. There was something special about playing college ball. The players were hungry, and the fans were loyal. It wasn't like in some markets, like Philly, where the fans turned on players as quickly as the wind changed directions. College football wasn't about the money—it was about the passion for the game.

The next step was going pro. My college playing days were numbered, and I would have to take the leap if I wanted to keep playing. *If... as if that was a question.* I'd never wanted to do anything else.

But nothing was guaranteed. Even if I made it a decade or more as a pro, what then? Life went on after football, and I would go crazy sitting on my ass for the rest of my life. I could go the Troy Aikman or Terry Bradshaw route and become a commentator, but if I was going to be on TV, I wanted a helmet on my head. The commentator role wasn't for me. So I needed to be prepared, and that included getting a degree. The time to do that was now.

I skidded to a stop in front of the geology building, having made it with two minutes to spare. That meant I had one minute and fifty-nine seconds to kill before taking my seat in the classroom. Though I loved college fans, I preferred them at a distance and not all up in my shit when I was only trying to stay awake while the professor explained the difference between metamorphic and sedimentary rocks. The man legitimately got excited about that shit. It was baffling. Normally, I was left alone in class, but normally, I wasn't in a class full of freshmen.

I slid into my seat as the TA dimmed the lights and turned on the PowerPoint for the day's lecture, which consisted of dozens of pictures of rocks. *Kill me now.*

I would much rather have been back in last year's philosophy class, having Katie hand my ass to me in a class discussion. I didn't know why that incident had stuck with me. Nothing else from the class had.

This date would be the distraction I needed.

CHAPTER 4

Katie

I MIGHT AS well have dealt with Kassidy, because my afternoon classes ended up being a waste anyway. I had never been one to be self-conscious, but I couldn't help but wonder if any of my classmates had witnessed the spectacle of the prior evening. It was ridiculous—there were nearly thirty thousand students on campus, so what were the odds? *Better than I would like to think about.* It was a college town, which meant downtown was the only nightlife around. But even if a classmate had seen me, chances were they would think nothing of it. Shenanigans and debauchery were part of college life, and my advertising my dating schedule was tame. But I'd made it a point not to draw attention to myself, and I'd broken my own number one rule.

Not only that, I was about to break it again. While it was doubtful anyone had paid much attention to me last night, being out on Wyatt's arm would certainly put me in the spotlight.

No, not me—him. As my professor waved his arms and pounded his fist on the lectern to drive home a point that I'd missed entirely, I exhaled. As usual, I was overreacting. People would notice Wyatt, but they wouldn't notice me. Their eyes would pass over me, and I would fade from their memories as soon as I entered them. Freddie Martin's girlfriend, Angela, was well-known because they'd been together forever. My one date with Wyatt would mean nothing in the long run.

The professor wrapped up his lecture, and my classmates started packing up their books and notebooks. I turned to the girl sitting behind me. "Did you take notes? I normally do, but I was really distracted today."

"Here." She flipped her binder open. "You can take a picture of them."

I smiled. "Thanks. I appreciate it."

"No problem."

Luckily, her handwriting was neat, and her notes seemed thorough. *Saved!*

Two more days until Friday, and I couldn't wait. The sooner I got my date with Wyatt over with, the sooner my life could get back to normal.

* * *

I PULLED THE elastic band out of my hair and let it fall onto my shoulders. Then I picked up my discarded highlighter and tried to focus on the borrowed notes I'd printed out. But it was useless. I couldn't focus, and my pounding head wasn't the only thing to blame. Kassidy's voice mail taunted me. Until I listened to it, my productivity would be zero.

Sighing, I pulled up the voice mail app on my phone and hit Play. I winced as her drunken voice screamed into my ear.

"Katie! Katelyn, my siiiisssstteerrr! Shhh... I'm talking to her right now. Well, not her, but her phone."

Oh, for the love... She'd drunk dialed me. It wasn't the first time, and it certainly wouldn't be the last. But what pissed me off was that I'd been stressing about her voice mail for twenty-four hours, and it had turned out to be nothing. Really, I couldn't blame that on her. I had chosen to put it off because I'd been afraid listening to it would be more distracting than not.

I crossed my arms over my chest as the message continued.

"You need to visit me. Hugh wants to meet you. He could totally hook you up. And we could do a project together, like old times!"

The voice mail abruptly ended, which was just as well. Her words were slurring so badly, I could barely understand her. Usually when that happened, she didn't even remember making the call. I had no idea who Hugh was, but whoever he was, I wasn't interested in anything he could offer me. I'd left that life behind and hadn't looked back.

The door to our apartment opened, and Destiny and Danielle came in, bringing with them the scent of freshly baked cookies. *Bless Dani.* She loved baking and usually brought over confections on our Wednesday TV nights, which had become a tradition when we'd all lived in the dorms freshman year.

I really needed to look over my notes since I hadn't heard a word of that afternoon's lecture, but my brain wasn't cooperating. Sometimes I studied while we watched, but I wouldn't be doing that tonight.

I joined my friends in the living room. Danielle had a naturally creamy complexion, but she looked pale, even for her.

"How are you feeling?" I asked.

"I threw up twice last night and once this morning." She grinned and held out a platter. "Cookie?"

I arched a brow, surveying the spread of chocolate chip, oatmeal, and white-chocolate macadamia nut. "How could you stomach baking after all that?"

She shrugged. "Cookies make everything better."

Destiny selected several cookies and plopped onto the couch. "Her cookies are making my ass wider."

Dani lifted her chin. "No one forces you to eat them. And you could always start running with me."

"That's a hell no."

Though Destiny claimed her ass was big, she was tall and had the build of a runway model. Plus, her metabolism was the stuff of legend. The rest of us were more than a little envious.

Rachel came out of the kitchen, carrying a huge bowl of popcorn. "What are we watching tonight?"

"It's my turn," Danielle said. "And I want to binge the first season of *Cali Girls*."

Closing my eyes, I exhaled. I'd dreaded this happening every week for the last three years, but so far, I'd gotten lucky. My luck was bound to run out eventually, and it looked like today was that day.

"Okay," I said way too brightly. "I'll queue it up. It's on Netflix, right?"

The girls were silent as I somehow managed to find the show without my hands shaking.

Rachel settled beside me on the couch and offered me the popcorn bowl. "Popcorn?"

"No, thanks. Not right now." My throat was too dry to swallow my spit, much less salty popcorn. As I pressed play to start episode one, I mentally calculated how long season one was—twelve episodes times forty-two minutes an episode equaled five hundred and four minutes. *Over eight hours.* Chances were the girls would want to finish the season next week, so between now and then, I would have to come up with an excuse to bail. For the moment, I would focus on getting through the next several hours.

The opening scene was followed by the show's catchy theme music and cameos of the cast while their names flashed on screen. And there she was staring at me—Kassidy Sterling.

Cali Girls, a high school drama set in California in the tradition of *90210* and *The O.C.*, had been her big break. Out of the entire cast, she'd been the only one who was actually young enough to be one of the high school students they were portraying. Despite that, the show marked her transition from a child star to an adult actor because it dealt with mature issues. *Cali Girls* was a far cry from the bubblegum *Sisters Squared*.

I wasn't knocking the tween sitcom. After all, the profits from the show were paying for my college education.

As Kassidy came on screen, I scrutinized her performance as I'd done many times before. Season one hadn't been her best work, but even still, she had that *something* that viewers loved, so they forgave her flatly delivered lines. By season two, her character, Lacey, had become the most popular on the show, and Kassidy's acting had immensely improved. Season three had granted her an Emmy nomination. When *Cali Girls* was canceled two years ago, fans had set up a website and taken donations in an attempt to revive the show.

What they didn't know was that Kassidy was the reason the show had ended. She'd wanted more—more money, but primarily, more fame. The small screen wasn't big enough for her anymore.

The funny thing was that the small screen had been way too big for me. Being half of *Sisters Squared* had suffocated me. I couldn't go anywhere without well-meaning fans crowding me, wanting to take pictures of me, wanting to *touch* me. The touching had really weirded me out. It was like they thought if their skin touched mine, something would rub off. What, though, I had no idea. Fame? Money? Beauty? It made no sense to me. Then again, as a child actor, I'd never known what it was like to be on the other side.

Our mother had been an aspiring actress, but when she'd gotten pregnant with us at age twenty, her career flatlined. It hadn't taken long for her to turn her sights to her adorable twin daughters. At six months old, Kassidy and I had started taking roles as babies in commercials and shows. We'd even made appearances in a few movies. When we were five, we were cast in *Kids Camp*, the most popular kids' show for over a decade. When we got too old for that, our mother negotiated a deal for our own show, and *Sisters Squared* was born. We even made two direct-to-TV *Sisters Squared* movies. It was always the two of us—the Sterling twins had been a package deal.

Until we weren't.

The first episode of *Cali Girls* ended, and Rachel hit pause before the next one could start. "Bathroom break," she said.

Destiny shoved the platter of cookies under my nose. "Eat more cookies, because if you don't, I'll end up eating them all before tomorrow."

I pushed the platter away. "No, thanks. My stomach still isn't right after last night."

That was only partially true. The primary reason my stomach was in knots was because I'd been staring at my sister's face for the last forty-two minutes, and though we were identical twins, it was like looking at a stranger. At sixteen, Kassidy had started altering her appearance. She'd started small, with lip injections, but before long, she'd succumbed to the pressures of Hollywood and gone under the knife.

In a way, she'd done me a favor. While she'd continued dying her hair blond, I'd let mine go back to its natural dark-brown color. She would rather be caught dead than be seen without makeup, and I sported a natural look. So between the hair, the makeup, and her facial augmentation, no one—not even my friends—connected the dots to realize that I had once been Katelyn Sterling, promising child star. Now I was just Katie Sullivan, college student.

Rachel returned and started the second episode. As I watched my twin, my stomach rolled. I hadn't seen her in three years, not since the brush with paparazzi made me realize that living a normal life meant more than giving up fame and fortune.

It also meant giving up my sister.

* * *

Wyatt

FUCK. IT WAS the only thought I had as I watched our local college news show. I didn't normally watch the half-baked show, but I couldn't tear my eyes away from the scene of a wannabe reporter accosting Coach Gurgin, asking if the rumors were true. Gurgin, being a class act, merely said "no comment" and moved on. But I knew the man well enough to recognize that his expression meant the reporter had gotten it right.

He was considering retirement, and the university had already put out feelers for a new head coach to start in the fall. I'd been blindsided on the field plenty of times, and this felt the same way.

Gurgin was not only the head coach, he was also the quarterback coach. I'd been scouted early in my high school career by a lot of other prominent teams, like Miami and Notre Dame, and it was Gurgin who'd convinced me to sign with Virginia Valley U. I hadn't questioned my decision until now. Because... *fuck!*

My position was secure—obviously—but I didn't want to deal with a new coaching staff my senior year. Gurgin was supposed to see me through.

The worst of it was finding out like this. Someone being considered for the head coach position had let it slip. It wasn't official, but of course the reporters had jumped all over that shit. A legendary coach leaving unexpectedly right after winning the national championship was big news in college football.

I picked up my phone and called Freddie. "Are you watching what I'm watching?"

"Not unless you're watching some stupid *Bachelorette* shit. *Ow!*" In the background, Angie yelled at him about calling her show stupid.

I rubbed the back of my neck. Normally, the bickering between those two amused me, but I wasn't in the mood for it. "Did you hear anything about Coach Gurgin retiring?"

"Are those rumors starting up again? You know better than to believe those. They start every off-season. I'm surprised we haven't heard before now."

I shook my head even though he couldn't see it. "This time it might be real." I told him what I'd seen on the news.

"Shit, man, that sucks." Though his words were heartfelt, he sounded detached, and it took me a minute to remember that it didn't affect Freddie. He wasn't going to be around next season, so while he might care for my sake, that was all it was.

"I gotta go." I hung up before Freddie could say anything else. I gripped the edge of my dresser so hard, I felt like there would be indents of my fingers when I let go.

I made a mistake.

For the first time, I seriously started doubting my decision to stay another year. My gut hadn't led me astray yet, but there was a first time for everything.

Coach Gurgin was one of the reasons I'd wanted to stay. Granted, that was a small reason and one I hadn't admitted even to myself before. But still, it was a reason. And now he might be leaving.

The betrayal stung. I straightened and stared at myself in the mirror. *Get it together.* Coach Gurgin didn't owe me anything. In his own words, he'd been cursed and blessed to be surrounded by women—his wife, three grown daughters, and two granddaughters so far—and his players were "his boys."

Hell, I'd considered myself his boy. But I guessed I'd read too much into the situation.

Goddammit, I hated being wrong. *If I even am wrong.* I didn't have the luxury of stewing over it now. I had a little over half an hour to shower and get to Katie's place. I'd been looking forward to seeing her again, to finding out if she was as interesting as she'd seemed in class last year. But now I was cursing myself for not letting her bail on me.

It served me right since I was breaking my own goddamned rule. I didn't date. One-night stands and flings? Sure. They weren't complicated, and everyone got a little something out of them. But lately those kinds of entanglements had become more trouble than they were worth. I was tired of evading the clutches of fame-seeking, money-hungry girls who only wanted the lifestyle the Archer might be able to provide for them. Freddie had known Angela since before he needed to shave, so he never had to question whether she wanted him or just FM4.

I picked up my phone and contemplated calling Katie and making up an excuse. But then I dropped it on the dresser and headed toward the shower. If I knew anything about women, then Katie was probably nearly ready, and I would be a jackass to cancel at this point.

God, I hoped she was as sharp and witty as I remembered.

CHAPTER 5

Katie

I STEPPED OUT of the shower and used my hand to wipe the condensation off the mirror. Normally, the glass stayed clear, but I'd taken a ridiculously long shower. The steam calmed me, and while I basked in the scalding water, the rest of the world didn't exist.

But now anxiety rushed through my bloodstream, sending a chill down my damp skin despite the steamy air. I hadn't been on a date in over a year, not since the beginning of my sophomore year. Anthony had been a senior, and after a month of dating, I was falling hard. So naturally, I'd had to end it, and it was then I'd decided I wouldn't date until I was done with college, until I was ready to be honest about my past. Keeping my secret meant any relationship I would have would be a sham, and that wouldn't be fair to anybody.

I conveniently overlooked the fact that I had also lied to my friends all these years.

I pulled a comb through my wet hair then tossed my head upside down so I could blow it dry. When I finished and righted myself, I ran my fingers through my dark locks. *Should I curl it?* I normally wore my hair straight or pulled into a ponytail. I couldn't remember the last time I'd done anything more to it.

"Now is not the time to start," I muttered. While I wanted to look nice—because *hello, who didn't?*—there was no reason to put in an extreme amount of effort. My date with Wyatt was an unfortunate obligation I'd roped myself into. Under no circumstances did I want to encourage a second date. Why he even wanted the first one when I'd given him an easy out was beyond me, but whatever. I would go, let him buy me dinner, then say goodnight, end of story.

So why had I dug out my special Urban Decay eye shadow palette instead of going with the standby Cover Girl? My eye shadow brush paused over the pan. *Screw it.* There was no point owning the stuff if I wasn't going to use it, and it wasn't as though I got many opportunities.

Twenty minutes later, I surveyed my handiwork in the mirror. I might have been six years out of the biz, but my makeup skills weren't as rusty as I'd thought they were. Eyebrows on point? Check. Smoky eye? Double check. Contoured cheekbones? Triple check. I hadn't spent all those years in a makeup chair without picking up some skills.

Now I had to figure out what to wear. It was February, which meant freezing in southwestern Virginia. Literally freezing. The high that day was only twenty-eight degrees. My closet was filled with designer dresses and skirts, but they were gifts from Kassidy, which meant they all had one thing in common—I would be lucky if my ass cheeks didn't fall out the bottom. She was generous when it came to gift-giving, but she didn't seem to understand what climate I was living in, or that slinky red-carpet-style clothing wasn't appropriate for wearing to class. But how could she know? Allowing her to visit me was out of the question.

Guilt struck me, but I shook it off. She'd chosen her path, and I'd chosen mine. It was as simple as that. Besides, she knew where I went to school. She could have looked up the weather. And for God's sake, she'd played a high school student on TV for years. She should've realized that college attire wasn't much different.

Shoved in the back of the closet, another gift from Kassidy caught my eye—black boots that went over the knee. The Italian leather was as smooth as a baby's bottom. The heels were so high and narrow, I could use them as weapons. With the ice on the ground, they were highly impractical, but I'd had them over a year and hadn't worn them yet. I pulled them out and stroked the leather. *Oh yeah.* These were definitely fuck-me boots.

I released my hold on the boots, and they fell to the floor. *What the hell? Fuck-me boots? Talk about sending the wrong message.*

But they were so nice, and they didn't deserve to gather more dust in the closet. I would compromise—I would wear them, but the rest of my outfit would be modest—dark skinny jeans and a black crew-neck sweater. The boots merely added a touch of sass. They didn't have to send any message I didn't want them to.

And I definitely didn't want to send a *fuck me* message, even if the Archer was much hotter in person than in any of the many recent photos I'd seen of him. I rarely got distracted in class, but it had been a struggle in the philosophy class I'd taken with him. He had an undeniable presence, whether he was completing sixty-yard passes or folding his huge, muscular form into a too-small desk.

This is crazy. I should not be going on a date with him. Even as the thought ran through my mind on repeat, I continued getting ready. When I pulled the smooth leather boots up my calves and slid the zippers up past my knees, that thought was replaced by another. *It would be a damn shame to let these boots go to waste.*

I checked myself out in the mirror from all angles, and damn if I didn't look hot. Not to toot my own horn, but I cleaned up pretty well when I put the effort in.

The only thing missing was earrings. I picked out a dangling sterling-silver pair that made a twinkling noise when I shook my head. *Perfect.*

I glanced at the clock and cursed. Ten minutes to spare. I'd timed my shower to give me exactly enough time to get ready without leaving any time for butterflies to take flight in my belly. Or so I'd thought. A lot of butterflies could worm their way out of their cocoons in ten minutes. I grabbed my purse to double-check that I had everything I needed since I didn't normally bother with one. Instead, I usually shoved my things in my backpack for going to campus.

There was a knock on the door, and I assumed it was Wyatt. He was early. *I like it.* Perhaps it made me a nerd, but punctuality was a turn-on.

Princess Buttercup, who had been asleep on my pillow, stood and arched her back. She gave me a nasty look, like it was my fault her slumber had been disturbed. Technically, it was, since Wyatt was there to see me, but whatever. The cat didn't pay rent, so she didn't have a right to complain. I allowed myself one last look in the mirror then went to the living room to answer the door.

Wyatt filled the doorway, blocking out the light from the dim light fixture in the foyer. He wore dark jeans, a parka, and a smolder. And God, he smelled good, like soap and forest. Instinctively, I leaned forward and inhaled deeply. I couldn't tell if he was wearing cologne or if it was just *him.*

The left side of his mouth stretched into a half-grin. *Oh shit.* Heat flooded my cheeks as I realized what I probably looked like with my neck extended and my nostrils sucking in his surrounding oxygen.

Suddenly, he gripped my elbow and moved me backward a few steps, coming into the apartment and closing the door behind him.

Him. The smell is definitely just him. Having sat near guys in class who doused themselves in cologne rather than showering—or so I assumed because I didn't know who else in their right mind used that much cologne—I could appreciate Wyatt's subtle, yet sexy scent.

He was still holding my arm, and we were standing close. With my heels on, my head came to the top of his chin, and I had to tilt my neck to look at him. Standing so close, I could see every inch of his chiseled jawline and full lips. My breath caught. He was better looking than he had any right to be. I was suddenly very glad I'd worn the fuck-me boots.

"Hi," I whispered. My knees threatened to buckle, and I was glad he was still holding on to me. But why hadn't he let go? *It's the boots... totally the boots.*

His eyes twinkled. "Your cat was trying to escape."

"Oh." So he hadn't been trying to put the moves on me. Feeling like an idiot, I stepped backward and nearly tripped over said cat.

Wyatt gripped my arms to steady me. *Damn, his hands are strong.* I nearly rolled my eyes at myself. *Of course they are.* He was nearly six and a half feet of pure muscle. It wasn't like he was going to have pansy hands. Still, I couldn't help but wonder what his hands would feel like on my arms without the sweater acting as a barrier between our skin.

"That's Princess Buttercup." I pulled my gaze away from his to shoot the furball a nasty look. "She's actually my roommate's cat."

"Cool." Pausing, he cocked his head. "You ready?"

"Oh, yeah. Sorry. I'm ready."

I stepped to the coat closet to grab my leather jacket, keeping an eye on Princess Buttercup the whole time. It would be like her to tangle herself in my ankles and knock me on my ass right in front of Wyatt. That was the kind of relationship the feline and I had.

As I followed Wyatt down the stairs and out to the parking lot, I cursed myself for breaking a cardinal rule of college dating—*always meet the guy at the restaurant*. Now I would be stuck on this date until Wyatt deemed it time to end. Letting him drive shifted the power dynamic in his favor. I guessed I could always come up with an excuse to escape and call an Uber. Or perhaps I was being mental. That was the most likely scenario.

Wyatt stopped next to an older Honda Accord parked in a visitor space. When he opened the passenger door for me, I blinked in surprise, not because he was being chivalrous, but because I hadn't expected him to be driving a sedan that had seen better days. I'd expected a flashy sports car. Except that wasn't right either. The image of him cramming his tall frame into the small classroom desk flitted through my mind. Perhaps a sleek, decked-out pickup truck would fit him better.

I realized he was staring at me expectantly. "Sorry," I muttered and lowered myself into the seat. Apparently, being around the Archer sent my senses running for the hills. When someone opened a car door for me, I was supposed to get into the vehicle, not stare at the upholstery like I was contemplating world peace.

I didn't know why I was wasting my time dissecting Wyatt Archer. My plan was to keep our date short and sweet... or maybe just short. Wyatt intrigued me, and that was not good. I hadn't spent the last six years hiding my true identity only to get tangled up with the most famous student on campus. Virginia Valley University was large, and that was one of the reasons I'd chosen it—so I could get lost in the crowd. By definition, dating Wyatt was not getting lost in the crowd. It was more like crowd-surfing.

Okay, perhaps I was being dramatic. *Leave the drama to Kassidy*, I chided myself.

As I fastened my seat belt, Wyatt closed the door and crossed to the driver's side. When he folded his body into the car, I realized my thought about the sports car was right. He would never be comfortable in one of those. I studied his profile as he started the car. The engine sputtered once before catching. A sports car wouldn't fit his personality anyway. While Wyatt was certainly good-looking, he wasn't a pretty boy. I decided the truck definitely fit in better with his personality—more rugged and able to take a beating.

"So..." I'd been silent for an awkwardly long amount of time. So had he, but he was driving, so one might argue that he was concentrating on the road. Still, he'd barely said anything since picking me up, and he was the one who'd insisted on this date. I'd tried to weasel out of it, but it seemed I would be responsible for conversation. "What are you majoring in?" It was probably the lamest question I could ask, but it was an easy one.

"Business management."

"Oh?" His response surprised me. I didn't know what athletes majored in, but I hadn't expected it to be a rigorous course of study. Of course, I already knew he was smart, so I shouldn't have been too surprised. "What do you plan to do with it?"

Wyatt chuckled, a deep reverberating sound that started in his chest. "Nothing anytime soon if I can help it."

"But you're not going in the draft this year, right?" I was enough of a fan to have read the list of players who were leaving the team in hopes of going pro. Wyatt's name wasn't there, and the entire university had released a collective sigh of relief. We were losing so many other players, though, that recapturing the magic of this year's season would be impossible. Even without the star players leaving, it would probably be impossible. The word "perfect" had been tossed around by newscasters about our team's season. It was a hell of a lot to live up to.

Wyatt's jaw tightened. "No." His tone was gruff, and his one-word response effectively closed that topic for conversation.

Alrighty, then. If he didn't want to talk about the draft, that was fine. But he didn't bother to begin another topic of conversation either. I studied him again, but reading him was about as easy as reading a blank concrete wall. He was one solid piece of nothingness.

Annoyance crept in. Aside from preventing Princess Buttercup's escape—and let's face it, I might not have cried about that—he hadn't done one thing to make me feel comfortable in his presence. He *had* opened the car door for me, but we were in the South, where a lot of guys had had that behavior ingrained into them at an early age.

"Why are you here?" I asked.

The blank wall turned into a guise of surprise as he glanced over at me. "What do you mean?"

"I gave you an out," I explained. "You didn't have to take me out tonight, so why are you?"

He was silent, and for a moment, I was worried I'd insulted him or hurt his feelings, and I wanted to suck my words back in.

"Why did you ask me out if you didn't want to go?" he asked finally.

"I was drunk, if you didn't notice."

"So you don't actually want to be here?"

"N-no," I stuttered. "That's not what I said."

"Kind of sounded like it to me."

He was right. *Damn.* I wondered if I was emitting an off-putting vibe.

"It's just that you haven't said much," I weakly explained.

He frowned. "I've got a lot on my mind."

Another reason he should have let me cancel. It didn't seem like he was in the mood to be pleasant company.

By the time we got to the restaurant, I was ready to fake an emergency and order myself an Uber. I hadn't wanted to go on this date because of Wyatt's level of fame, but now I wanted to escape his sullen mood.

Wyatt parked, and I let myself out of the car. He trotted around the hood to my side.

"Sorry," he said. "I was going to get that for you."

"I'm capable of letting myself out of a car," I retorted.

A slow grin crept across his face, and I got the feeling he found me amusing. "No doubt. But most girls like it when guys open doors for them."

Most girls... He would know. I blew out a breath and rubbed my arms as the cold seeped through my clothes and down to my bones. *This is a disaster.*

He offered his arm. "Come on."

I stared at his arm and was tempted to ignore the gesture, but that wouldn't have been smart with these heels. Besides that, I was coming across as a bitch, which wasn't my intention. I hooked my arm around his, and he guided me toward the door.

Flavio's was a small, locally owned Italian restaurant that was housed in a building that had started out as a Wendy's. They'd spruced up the inside, though, and now it was one of the nicer places to eat in our small town. I loved Italian food and couldn't remember the last time I'd been there. It wasn't the type of place I went to with the girls.

Once inside, we were greeted by Flavio himself. Flavio was an older gentleman straight from Italy, but despite this being his restaurant, he couldn't even boil spaghetti. Or so I'd read in an interview.

He smiled at us. "Welcome, welcome! Party of two?"

Wyatt nodded. "There should be a reservation under Archer."

In the dining room, two servers had stopped what they were doing to gawk at Wyatt. Instinctively, I shifted so that his body blocked their view of me.

Wyatt looked down at me then followed my line of sight to the two servers. "Flavio, is there any chance you have a private table?"

I had to give him credit for not only noticing my discomfort, but for taking action.

Flavio looked over his shoulder at his employees and barked something in Italian. The two girls blushed and hurried about their duties. The older man turned back to us. "Signore Archer, let me set something up for you."

"Thank you, sir," Wyatt said respectfully. "I appreciate it." He guided me to a corner of the lobby, where the view from the dining room was obscured.

"How do you stand it?" I asked.

He shrugged. "Goes with the territory."

"It's like living in a fishbowl." I didn't know if I was referring to his current existence or if I was reminiscing about my own time in the spotlight. Either way, I wanted no part of it.

"Yeah, but I'm a big fish in a little pond right now," he said. "It won't be this way when I go pro."

I arched a brow. "Really? You think Tom Brady doesn't get attention wherever he goes?"

Wyatt's mouth stretched into the lazy smile that I was quickly growing fond of. "Are you comparing me to Tom Brady?"

"He's a famous quarterback. You're a famous quarterback."

"Not really. If I quit playing tomorrow, no one would remember me in five years."

I frowned. "I don't think that's true."

"Fame has a very limited shelf life," Wyatt said. "Trust me on that."

He seemed so certain. My instinct was to prove him wrong, but my evidence was of the personal nature, so I let the matter rest.

Flavio reappeared with a smile on his face. "Signore and Signora, please follow me."

CHAPTER 6

Wyatt

I GESTURED FOR Katie to walk ahead of me. She'd taken her jacket off, and I gave it a valiant effort to keep my eyes off her ass. Well, honestly, I didn't put too much effort into it. Her ass was tight, round, and perfect.

She glanced at me over her shoulder, and I dragged my gaze up to her face. One dark eyebrow arched, and I knew I'd been busted. Grinning, I winked. She twisted her neck back around and flipped her hair over her shoulder.

"Right in here." Flavio led us into a small room off the kitchen. It looked like a dining room that would be in someone's house with a large table that sat ten. Two places had been set at a corner of the table.

Flavio motioned for us to sit. "Is this good?"

I held my hand out, and Flavio gripped it. "Perfect. Thank you."

The older man nodded, pleased. "Your server will be in shortly."

Katie draped her jacket on the back of her seat and sat before I could pull the chair out for her. My grandfather opened every door my grandmother walked through and pulled out every chair she sat in. He was an old-school gentleman, and when I was twelve, he'd sat me down and given me the talk. Not *that* talk, but the one where he explained how to treat a woman.

I hadn't always abided by his teaching, but something about Katie made me remember his words.

Flavio picked up the menus on the table, opened them, and placed them in our hands. "Enjoy." He slipped out.

We spent a few moments looking over our menus. While soft music was playing in the main dining room, our private space was silent. It might have been awkward, except I very rarely felt self-conscious about anything. It was a pointless emotion, and one I'd stripped out of my wheelhouse long ago.

"So, um, what's good here?" Katie peeked at me over the top of the large menu.

"Have you never been?"

"It's been a while," she muttered.

I stared at her for a beat, wondering about the meaning behind her words. Did that mean she hadn't dated in a while? Because Flavio's was one of the few restaurants in town that was good for a date. I forced the speculation from my mind. It wasn't my business, and it wasn't like me to read into things. I took people at their word, which meant they sure as hell better say what they meant.

"The cannolis are good."

She chuckled. "Are we starting with dessert?"

The edge of my mouth lifted. "If that's what you want."

She blushed at my double entendre. The pink on her cheeks looked good on her. I took a moment to study her. She looked different tonight. Maybe it was the makeup—she was wearing more of it. While I was pleased she'd taken the time to do herself up for our date, she hadn't needed to bother—she was gorgeous either way.

Our server arrived, and thankfully, she wasn't one of the girls who'd been gawking and made Katie uncomfortable. The server listed the specials, presented us with a wine menu, then discreetly left so we could make our decisions.

I offered the wine list to Katie. "You want to look at this?"

She shook her head. "I'm not actually a big drinker."

"Really?" I gave her a quizzical look and gestured to the space between us. "Isn't that how this happened?"

She shifted in her seat, obviously uncomfortable. She opened her mouth to speak, shut it, then cocked her head. "Seriously, why didn't you let me cancel? I've been wondering. I'm not your type."

Not liking where this conversation was heading, I leaned back in my chair and crossed my arms. "What's my type?"

She shrugged. "I don't know. Not me."

It took me a second to read between the lines and figure out what the real deal was. "What you mean is *I'm* not *your* type."

"What?" She shook her head. "That's not what I said."

"You didn't say it, but that doesn't mean it's not true."

I thought she was going to deny it, but instead, she sighed. "Okay, I admit it. You're not my type."

Her words delivered an unexpected punch to my gut, but I shook it off. "Then why did you ask me out?"

She threw her hands up. "I tried to cancel!"

I leaned forward. "And that's why I wouldn't let you. Aside from one very unfortunate case of the stomach flu, I've never had a girl bail on me."

"And what?" She seemed annoyed. "You want to keep your perfect record?"

Shit. I hadn't meant to make myself sound like an asshole. "That's not what I said."

She smirked. "It's kind of irritating when people put words into your mouth, isn't it?"

The date was going downhill fast. When I'd picked her up, I was in a crappy mood, and she'd understandably reacted to that. Now we were playing aggressive verbal ping-pong, but my mood had actually improved. Most girls nodded and smiled, going along with whatever I wanted.

They tried to transform themselves into what they thought I wanted, which meant they showed a lot of skin and acted like airheads. I hadn't dated much, but it was fair to say that probably *had* been my type. I didn't have time for anything that required thought, especially during the season.

Katie definitely required thought. I liked it.

I smiled. "You're not my type, and that's exactly why I'm here."

* * *

Katie

HE WAS MESSING with me. That had to be it.

I put my hands on the edge of the table, prepared to push my chair back and leave his ass at the Thanksgiving-dinner-sized table. I would rip these fuck-me books off my feet and walk home if I had to.

His hands clasped over mine. "Wait. I'm sorry. Whatever I did to piss you off, I'm sorry." Mild alarm crossed his features. With his perfect record, I guessed he'd never had a girl walk out on him. I also got the feeling he wasn't too experienced with apologizing. The words seemed foreign to him, but his expression was earnest. Maybe I was being too hard on him.

Exhaling, I settled back in my chair. I had flown off the handle because I was on edge, which wasn't fair to him. If he'd been any other guy, I wouldn't have been looking for a reason to escape. Of course, if he'd been any other guy, I wouldn't have let myself get dared into asking him out in the first place.

"No, I'm sorry," I said. "This whole situation is weird for me."

"Why?" He seemed perplexed.

"You're the Archer. You're famous." That was all I could say without getting into my sob story of being a former child star. *No, thank you.* That was one story Wyatt would never be privy to. If I could erase those years from my autobiography, I would.

He might take my words to mean I was intimidated by him, but that was far from the truth. I'd been in the company of much more famous people. But the thing was that I didn't want to be in the company of any type of fame.

Wyatt chuckled, and I felt the deep sound in my belly— it vibrated off my organs and settled somewhere much lower. *God, he's sexy.*

"I'm really not."

My eyes widened, and it took me a second to realize that he was responding to what I'd said instead of what I'd been thinking. *Thank God.* Because I hadn't embarrassed myself enough. I shoved all thoughts of how sexy Wyatt was from my mind and sternly told my lady bits to calm the eff down.

I tapped a finger on my chin. "Isn't your larger-than-life picture on a billboard outside of campus?" My question stopped his laughter, which had been my intention.

"That's not about me. It's about the team."

"But it's still you. You're the face of the team."

He shifted in his seat. "So is Freddie."

"So you admit you're the face of the team?"

"Well, I'm the quarterback."

I smiled. "I'm right. It's okay. You can admit it." *Victory is mine.*

His eyes locked onto mine. His expression was somewhere between smug and teasing, but I never found out if he would have let me win the argument because the server appeared to take our orders. Damn... I hadn't even looked at the menu. I let Wyatt order first and quickly scanned the entrees to make a selection.

When the server had gone, Wyatt rested his forearms on the table. "You know, most girls find the fame thing a turn-on."

I was definitely turned on, but his fame had nothing to do with it.

"I'm not most girls," I muttered. Most girls hadn't had their thirteenth birthday parties crashed by paparazzi.

"That's what I meant earlier," he explained. "You're not the usual type of girl who comes on to me."

I stared at him, trying to get a read on him, but his expression was neutral. I guessed that was one of the things that made him a good quarterback—his opponents couldn't read him. But that just made him a frustrating date.

"Is that a good thing?" I asked finally.

He cocked his head. "What do you think?"

I thought back to the redhead who had practically been sitting in his lap at the bar, the one I'd shooed away. He hadn't seemed to mind her attention, but he hadn't been heartbroken that she'd left either. "Yes?" The word came out as a question.

He laughed, the sound hitting me deep in the gut again. "Yes," he confirmed.

"But you date those girls."

He shrugged. "Yeah."

"But..." I didn't understand him. He was a walking contradiction. "Why?"

"Why not?"

Stunned, I blinked. I didn't have an answer to that question, but luckily, he didn't seem to expect one. Shaking my head, I laughed.

He grinned. "I'm glad I amuse you." Though the words themselves could have been taken harshly, I could tell he didn't mean them that way. As much as I hated to admit it, Wyatt did amuse me—except *amuse* wasn't the right word.

Because of my time in class with him, I'd already known he wasn't a dumb jock. Still, there was more to him than I'd realized before.

That scared me because I wanted to peel off his layers and find out what made him tick. And let's face it—peeling off his layers of clothing would not be a sacrifice.

I straightened, squared my shoulders, and leaned back against my chair, putting as much distance between us as possible. He noticed the shift in my posture immediately, and the grin slid off his face.

It hurt my heart a little.

Damn it.

I liked what I knew of him so far, which had sent my walls sky high. I never should have asked him out, but I had, and I was with him now. I knew better than anyone that beneath the fame was a real person, and I had momentarily forgotten that. *He is not his fame.* Still, I couldn't have one without the other. I of all people understood that.

Leaning on the table, I cocked my head. "Can we start over? I feel like we got off on the wrong foot."

"Good idea." He ran a hand along the back of his neck in a sheepish manner. "That was my fault." The action made him look less ruggedly handsome and more boyish. *But still, oh so attractive.*

I thought back to what he'd said in the car about having a lot on his mind and how he'd clammed up at the mention of the draft. *Of course he had.* Deciding to declare for the draft—or not, in his case—had to be one of the most important decisions a college player made. I was surprised he wasn't going pro, especially since FM4 was.

"No worries," I said casually. "You've got a lot on your plate."

He rubbed his fingers on his forehead, along his hairline, causing his cowlick to stick up, which only added to his newfound boyish charm. "Do you ever feel like you're fucking up no matter what you do? That no decision is the right one?"

His question hit close to home. When I'd called it quits on acting, Kassidy and my mom had been devastated. I liked to tell myself they were upset that I was essentially cutting myself out of their lives, but deep down, I knew the truth—the Sterling twins were more marketable as a set. By herself, Kassidy was only another child actor trying not to fade into obscurity as she transitioned to adulthood. My sister had always been the more immature of the two of us, and she didn't understand why I didn't want the same thing as her. Once she moved past that, she didn't understand why I wouldn't keep up the charade for her sake. She'd called me selfish.

My mom hadn't been on board with my early retirement, to put it mildly. She was a momager who was losing one of her charges—and half of her source of income. Luckily, when my parents divorced two years previously, the judge had granted them joint custody, so I was able to live with my dad. At first, I didn't think my mom would let us live in peace, but after Dad had a long conversation with her, he assured me she wouldn't bother us.

Maybe he'd talked some sense into her. Most likely, he'd bribed her.

I didn't even want to know.

The truth was I'd enjoyed acting. Getting lost in a role and immersed in someone else's story had been exhilarating, and I'd been good at it. I would have kept going if I could have lived a normal life once the cameras stopped rolling, but it didn't work like that, especially with the way my mom had been running my career.

I met Wyatt's eyes. "Yes. I know exactly what that's like."

He studied me for a moment, and as he did, the gold in his irises mesmerized me. There was so much more to this boy than met the eye, and suddenly, staying out of the spotlight didn't seem as important as digging beneath the facade Wyatt presented to the world.

Slowly, he reached for my hand. Taking it in his, he held it up and inspected my fingertips. My breath caught. The action itself was innocent, but I knew in that moment that there would never be anything innocent about the way his skin felt touching mine.

He paused in his inspection of my fingers to meet my gaze. "I believe you do know."

My lips parted. My instinct was to use our joined hands to yank him toward me so I could discover if the feel of his lips on mine would be as sensual as his touch. His fingers were tracing mine so intently, it was like he was trying to memorize the pattern of my fingerprints. Sportscasters waxed poetic about his intensity on the field, but they had no freaking idea.

Our server appeared with our salads, and Wyatt released my hand so she could place the dishes on the table. Looking away, I cleared my throat and silently thanked my lucky stars that we'd been interrupted before I'd done something foolish like offered to have his babies.

Perhaps I needed to rethink my no-dating policy so that I wasn't on the verge of humiliating myself the second a handsome guy paid me some attention. But even as the thought entered my mind, I knew that Wyatt wasn't just some handsome guy. If he were, then I wouldn't have the feeling in the pit of my stomach that I was in big, big trouble.

CHAPTER 7

Wyatt

ONCE KATIE AND I got over the fucktastic weirdness that had plagued the beginning of our date, we relaxed into a rhythm—friendly but sharp banter until I inevitably said something to make her blush.

I lived for making this girl blush.

With pink-tinged cheeks, she shifted from beautiful to cute, and somehow that made her even more appealing. Though I didn't know how that was possible. Katie pushed all of my buttons, and I was left in the unfamiliar terrain of not wanting to fuck things up.

Maybe it made me sound like an asshole, but I'd never really given a shit before. Girls came and went, and there was always another one in the endless line. They were interchangeable, and I'd learned back in high school to take advantage of the symbiotic relationship.

Katie wasn't like that. For starters, she wasn't looking to be seen on the arm of the Archer. Just the opposite, in fact. And the idea that she was interchangeable was laughable. Katelyn Sullivan—*Katie*—was one of a kind.

As the server cleared our dirty plates, I winked at Katie, earning the blush I sought. "Dessert?"

She put her hands over her belly. "I don't think so. I ate way too much, but it was so good."

"How about a rain check, then?"

She nodded. "Definitely."

Exhaling, I relaxed my shoulders. *Loser.* I was totally fishing to see if she would be interested in a second date. Even though the second half of our evening was going well after our rough start, I wasn't sure she would want to see me again. But I definitely wanted to see her again.

Hell, I didn't want to stop being with her tonight, but she'd already declined dessert. I loved living in a college town, but at times like this, it kind of sucked. It was cold as balls outside, so I couldn't suggest we go for a walk somewhere. Other than frat parties and going to bars downtown, there wasn't much else to do. I could invite her back to my house to watch a movie, but all the "Netflix and chill" memes had taken that option off the table. There was no good way to extend our date without involving loud drunk people or leading her to think all I wanted was to get into her panties.

Okay, I did want to get into her panties. She was smoking hot, and I was a red-blooded male, but I wanted more than that—I wanted to get into her head. Like I'd said—unfamiliar territory.

I didn't think too deeply on how shallow that made me.

After I paid the check—and fought off her argument that she should pay since she'd technically asked me out—I helped her slip into her leather jacket, earning yet another blush. I got the impression that not many men had done that for her, so she was a little awkward with it, but that only made me like her more. I rested my hand lightly on the small of her back to guide her out of the restaurant, and I wished yet again that it weren't winter. If she weren't wearing a coat, I would be able to feel her through her shirt. As she walked slightly ahead of me, I almost resisted the urge to check out her ass again. My gentlemanly behavior only took me so far, and she had an ass that deserved to be worshiped.

In the vestibule, one of the servers who'd stared at us when we entered was waiting with a football and a Sharpie. She held it out to me as we passed. "I hope you don't mind. I used my dinner break to run out and get this. It's for my little brother. He's a big fan."

I wanted to grind my teeth, but instead I smiled and took my hand off Katie's back to accept the ball and marker. Katie quietly stepped aside to wait.

"Oh yeah?" I played along. "What's his name?"

"Connor." She spelled it for me. "He's twelve."

I personalized the autograph and passed the ball back to her.

"Thank you so much." She beamed. "This will mean so much to him."

"No problem. Have a nice night."

Katie pushed open the door and exited into the cold. I followed.

I tried to imagine twelve-year-old Connor's excitement at receiving the ball, but I couldn't picture it. I wasn't Peyton Manning or Joe Montana. I was only a college football player, like my dad had been. The server—I hadn't bothered to ask her name or read it off her name tag—would have done better to hunt down Freddie and get him to sign the ball. Next year, FM4 was bound to be making headlines as Rookie of the Year.

As I opened the passenger door for Katie, I scowled. For the past hour, I'd managed to forget about the draft, Coach Gurgin, about all of it. I wasn't normally prone to worry or stress—those two things denoted a lack of confidence, and I had plenty of that to spare. I'd been a great high school quarterback, and I was an even better college quarterback. The higher the level of competition, the more focused I became. Many considered football to be a thuggish sport, full of meatheads and violence. But it wasn't—it was about taking your opponent's measure, finding their weaknesses, and using our team's strengths to come out on top.

I'd weighed all the factors in deciding my next step, and I'd thought I made the best decision. But in a way, inaction had been my decision, the status quo. Was I taking the easy road instead of the risky one?

Being unsure of myself was an uncomfortable and unfamiliar feeling, not one I wanted to get used to.

Pausing next to the driver's side door, I wiped a hand down my face, taking my scowl with it. I didn't want to end this date the way it had begun. Taking one last deep breath, I lowered myself into the car.

"Does that happen a lot?" Katie asked.

I shrugged. "Sometimes. Not really. I don't know." I sounded like an idiot, but I didn't know what would be considered a lot because it had always been my reality. Even in high school, I had been treated like royalty. The shit I'd gotten away with was ridiculous.

She traced her finger along the seam of the fabric on the edge of her seat. "I was just wondering because no one seemed to bother you in class or at the bar." She paused. "At least, not to ask for an autograph."

"The professors are usually pretty good about making sure student athletes aren't bothered in class," I explained, thinking about the exception of my geology professor. "And most people who want autographs are too intimidated to come up to me downtown, especially if there's a group of us."

"Yeah, I guess it would be kind of lame to ask for an autograph in the middle of TOTS. Nerd alert, right?" She chuckled.

"Yeah." I pulled the seat belt across my chest and started the car. "But I'm really not as big of a celebrity as you seem to think I am. Take me off campus, and I'm not that big of a deal."

"You're not giving yourself enough credit."

I laughed. She had no idea how much credit I gave myself—I knew I was the best college quarterback in the country. But that would be over soon, and none of it would matter if I couldn't deliver on the professional field. I'd mastered my play at the college level, but what if it wasn't enough? What if *I* wasn't enough?

My laugh ended abruptly. Damn, I did not like this new insecure side of myself. I'd never doubted my abilities before, just the timing of when to take the next step.

Out of the corner of my eye, I noticed Katie looking at me, and I realized I hadn't responded other than to laugh. "Don't worry about me. There's a reason I've been called cocky once or twice."

"And are you?"

A few minutes ago, I could have brushed off the question with my usual cocky-confident explanation, but now I wasn't so sure. "I hope not," I said honestly.

"I think you have to be a little cocky to do what you do."

Her comment shocked the shit out of me. I'd always thought the same thing, but I didn't know how to explain it without sounding like an ass. She really seemed to understand the mind-set.

"A lot of big players are humble," I said.

"Sure, in public," she allowed. "But it takes a lot of balls to go out on the field in front of millions and play like that. I don't see how anyone could do that without being at least a little cocky."

"Maybe, but some players tune out the noise." I didn't know why I was arguing with her since I agreed with everything she was saying. I guessed I just liked the back-and-forth.

She shrugged. "Only those who aren't at the top of their game can do that forever."

"What do you mean?" I took a left on the road that led to her apartment complex. We were nearing her place too soon. I wanted to keep hearing her thoughts about the game that had become my life.

"Even if you can tune out the crowd while you're on the field, what about when you're off the field?" She turned toward me. "There are press conferences and requests for autographs, maybe some charity and community service events. There are certain responsibilities that come with being the best that can't be ignored."

Her analysis stunned me. She understood the life I was walking into more than anyone outside of the game should.

"Talking to the press is in the players' contracts," I said. "So that part is definitely unavoidable."

She nodded. "I didn't realize that, but it makes sense. At the end of the day, it's a business. Media helps with exposure, which leads to more money. It always comes down to money." Her expression darkened, and I wondered why she spoke so passionately about the subject.

I would be crazy to play football only for the money. There were too many risks and long-term consequences for that. I would play regardless, but the money helped. I wasn't getting paid now, but without the scholarship, I doubted I would be at VVU. Neither my grandparents nor my father had tuition money lying around. Hell, they'd barely been able to scrape together enough cash to buy me my piece-of-crap car junior year of high school. I wouldn't have had a problem busting my ass working nights and weekends like some of my high school buddies, except football hadn't left time for that. Even in the off-season, I was constantly training.

"Some people think college athletes should be paid," I said. "What's your opinion on that?"

She paused, seeming to consider it. "I haven't really thought about it before. I don't know enough to offer an informed opinion. But I guess the school makes a lot of money off the team, right?"

I nodded, though I tended not to think about that. Even if I wanted to take a stand to change the no-compensation policy, I wouldn't have the time without sacrificing my performance on the field or giving up what little social life I had. So I didn't think about it. It was what it was.

I pulled into a guest parking spot and turned off the ignition. I hopped out of the car and got around to the passenger's side as Katie was opening the door.

"Careful." I took hold of her arm. "There could be black ice." There wasn't, but I wanted the excuse to hold her close to me as we walked to her building.

"Thanks." She swallowed, and her fingers gripped the strap of her purse. Her body shivered. Though she looked hot in her black leather jacket, it was impractical for winter in Bleaksburg. The wind was killer, cutting through clothing and freezing the bones. I tucked her under my arm and pulled her close to my body. She let out an involuntary sigh of relief.

She was slender—not skinny, but slender. Through her jacket, I could tell she was toned. I wondered what she did to maintain her body, if she simply worked out or played a sport. Was she the type to push her body for vanity's sake, or did she relish the burn of her muscles as they worked?

She leaned into me as the wind picked up speed, and I caught a whiff of her hair. It smelled like some kind of flower.

Holy fuck. I'd never been happier my parka covered my crotch. I shoved my free hand in my pocket to subtly readjust myself.

Katie's apartment was on the third floor, but I stopped at the base of the stairs. She was on the first step before she realized I'd halted. Turning, she gave me a quizzical look.

Normally, I would walk her to her door, but if I went up to the third floor with her, I didn't trust myself not to beg to be invited in.

Hell, normally I and whatever chick I was hooking up with would be stumbling drunk by the time we got to her apartment, and there would never be a question of whether I was coming in.

The memory of all those cheap nights made me take a step back, putting some distance between Katie and me. God, I was so into this chick, and I didn't want things to end up like every other time with every other girl.

With her on the step and me on the ground, our heights were closer to even, though I still towered several inches above her. Our bodies were perfectly aligned for me to yank her to me and grind against her.

I closed my eyes for a moment and called to mind every tip my grandfather had ever given me about how to treat a woman. But all of the blood was leaving my brain in favor of heading south. I could barely remember how to breathe, much less recall teachings I'd never thought I would need.

Fuck it. I slipped my arm under her jacket and around her waist then pulled her against me. Her eyes widened in surprise. Our faces were only inches apart.

"I had a good time tonight," I said quietly, resisting the urge to use the cheap move of licking my lips, which in the past had driven girls wild.

Her eyes searched my face, but she was still, waiting for me to make the next move. It took all the willpower I had to play it cool, to not turn into a Neanderthal, throw her over my shoulder, and cart her sweet ass up to her apartment.

Her lips parted, and all gentlemanly thoughts flew out of my head. Hungrily, I went for her lips, checking myself at the last second to rein it in.

I sucked her lower lip between mine and stifled a groan as my cock pulsed. Her hands went to my shoulders, but other than that, she was frozen in place. If not for her erratic breathing, I would have questioned whether my kiss was welcome. Then she let out a sigh, and I was nearly undone.

I wanted so much more. I wanted to strip off her foolish leather jacket and lick every inch of her skin. I wanted to memorize every curve of her figure. I wanted to count every freckle on her body.

Pulling myself away, I took her hand and pressed her fingertips to my lips. "Dream of me, Katie." Because I sure as hell would be dreaming of her.

Her eyes, which had been half-closed, opened wide, and her lips parted in surprise. Her reaction insanely pleased me.

"Okay," she whispered.

After one last kiss on her fingertips, I walked away.

CHAPTER 8

Katie

AS WYATT WALKED away, I gaped. Then I put my fingers to my lips. *What the hell just happened?*

I'd been so busy debating whether to ask him up that it had taken longer than it should have for me to realize he was leaving. *Wait, what?* I didn't understand what was happening. Was he letting me down easy? A thanks, but no thanks? I guessed my fuck-me boots didn't deserve that title after all.

Even when I lost sight of him, I stupidly stood there, staring at the path he'd taken to his car. The wind whistled as it blew past, snapping me out of my daze. I turned on my heel and trotted up the stairs to my apartment.

Rachel was lounging on the couch with a book in the living room. She fumbled her book, and it crashed to the floor as she sat up straight with a wicked grin on her face. Then she frowned. "Wait, where's Wyatt?"

I turned my back to her to hang my coat in the closet. "I don't know."

"Why not? I thought..."

Turning, I crossed my arms and narrowed my eyes at her. "You thought he was a sure thing?"

She had the good graces to blush. "Well, yeah."

"Rach, come on. Did you really think I was going to sleep with him?" I asked the question like I knew with certainty what the answer was, but the truth was if Wyatt had continued kissing me like that, I didn't know what I would have done.

I unzipped the stupid boots and stepped out of them. They were a mistake. I felt silly for having worn them.

Rachel shrugged. "It would be good for you. When was the last time you were with someone?"

"I'm not going to answer that." Primarily because I would have to do some serious math, and it was too late on a Friday night for that. But mostly because I didn't want a lecture on how I should loosen up. I'd been half a second away from loosening up with Wyatt, but apparently I didn't meet his standards. *Time for a subject change.* "I thought you were going out with Adam tonight."

She scowled. "He blew me off. Asshole."

I shook my head. "Why do you bother with him?"

"It's easy."

She and Adam had been on-again, off-again for the last two years. Lately, though, they'd been more off than on. I didn't have a strong opinion about the guy, mainly because, even after two years, he'd never bothered getting to know me or any of Rachel's friends.

"You deserve more."

Rachel acted indifferent, but deep down, she wanted the kind of love found in a romantic comedy. The trouble was she was too much of a realist to hope it could actually happen.

She waved a hand. "Yeah, yeah." Then she pounced on me in a fair imitation of Princess Buttercup. "Tell me about your date."

I groaned. Thought I didn't particularly approve of her "relationship" with Adam, I wished he hadn't chosen that night to blow her off. I could have used some time to decompress before the inevitable cross-examination.

"We went out to dinner, and he brought me home."

Rachel glared at me.

I laughed. "Okay, fine. We went to Flavio's."

She waited a beat then threw her hands up in exasperation. "That's it? That's all you're going to give me?"

There was so much I could tell her, from Wyatt's gentlemanly habit of opening doors to the ungentlemanly look in his eyes when he'd said goodbye. Thinking about the way his body had felt pressed against mine—hard, powerful, strong—made my body respond.

But then he'd left so abruptly. In a way, that had made things easy on me because it had taken the decision of inviting him in out of my hands. *Thank God.* I was pretty sure I would have asked him in. And if those boots had been a mistake, getting horizontal with Wyatt would have been an even bigger one. It was better this way, yet a glum feeling washed over me.

Was I... *disappointed*? Holy crap, I was. I was totally disappointed not to be naked with the Archer right that very second. Except, if I'd asked him in, I doubted we would be naked already, especially with Rachel there. I couldn't decide if that was good or bad.

Wyatt was making me totally mental, but all I could think about was what it would have been like to be pressed against him without layers of winter clothing in the way.

"Hello?" Rachel waved her hand in front of me. "Earth to Katie. What else?"

"What else?" I echoed, snapping out of my wicked thoughts. "The mushroom ravioli was amazing."

A pillow smashed into my face, knocking me backward. If I hadn't been distracted by imagining what Wyatt's V muscle looked like, I would have been able to deflect it. *See? Thinking about him is bad for my health.*

"Ugh!" Rachel exclaimed. "You're in danger of losing your BFF title. You know that, right?"

Laughing, I tossed the pillow back to her. "I don't kiss and tell."

She squealed. "You *kissed* him?"

Heat spread to my cheeks as I remembered the sensation of him sucking on my lower lip. *Mistake, mistake, mistake. Remember, it would have been a mistake to invite him up.*

"It was more like he kissed me."

She gripped my knees. "Did you kiss him back?"

Did I? I had been too shocked to do more than stand there like an idiot. So I couldn't say that I had indeed kissed him back, but I'd been receptive to the kiss. *Right?* Groaning, I put my head in my hands. Maybe that was why he had left.

"Well? Did you?" Rachel asked with alarm.

"I don't want to talk about it."

She stared at me for a moment then crossed her arms with a smirk. "You like him."

I looked up sharply. "What?"

My bestie nodded knowingly. "You do. That's why you won't talk about it."

I scoffed. "That's crazy." What I meant was *I'm crazy.* Because fuck if I didn't like him. That wasn't part of the plan. The date was supposed to be a one-and-done to show my friends I wasn't a total lame-a-zoid.

She shook her head. "It's not. If you didn't care, you'd spill all the juicy details."

"Who says the details are juicy?" I was teasing her, but the truth was the details weren't nearly as juicy as I would have liked.

She blew out an exasperated breath. "Fine. All the embarrassing, boring, juicy, or *whatever* details."

I opened my mouth to protest but clamped it shut as I wracked my memory for an example to prove her wrong. I came up blank.

My phone buzzed, giving me a momentary respite from her questioning. When I fished it out of my purse, my heart fell a little when I saw it was only a text from my dad and not Wyatt.

Stupid. I didn't know where Wyatt lived. He could still be driving home. Or he could be at a bar downtown for all I knew. But besides those practical reasons, it was silly to think he would have texted me already, if he even texted me at all. For all I knew, our date was a one-time deal.

Funny how my tune had changed in the last few hours. Rachel was right. I cared. *Damn it.* Sighing, I opened the text from my dad. "Shit."

"Is everything okay?" Rachel's teasing tone was gone and replaced with one of concern.

I stood. "Just some family business," I muttered. "Don't worry." I shuffled off to my bedroom before opening the link my dad had sent me with the line, *I thought you should hear this from me first.*

The link took me to a celebrity gossip site. Front and center was a picture of Kassidy getting out of a Corvette. She was obviously drunk. Lipstick was smeared on her face, and her legs were splayed open for the world to see. The site didn't have the decency to blur the area and instead showed her lady business to the entire world.

I cringed. My dad should not have to see his daughter like that. Though he had little contact with her because of the tension between him and my mom, she was still his child.

The next picture was of her and an up-and-coming actor, Tate Hughes. Their arms were wrapped around one another as they stumbled along the sidewalk. As I peered at the picture, I noticed Kassidy's dark-red lipstick staining the collar of his shirt and the flap over the zipper on his pants.

"For fuck's sake, Kassidy," I muttered. The pictures were damning enough. I didn't know if I would be able to stomach the article. I wanted to tuck my phone away and forget about it, but my dad was right. It was better that I knew before I came across the story unaware.

The article contained a lot of the usual stuff, including a summary of Kassidy's transition from a child star. There was a brief mention of how I'd disappeared from the limelight as well as a picture from our days on *Sisters Squared.* The next part was new, though. I'd been so focused on Kassidy's train wreck that I hadn't realized the article was the latest in the series about momagers who'd led their children astray.

The final line filled me with rage. *Maybe Kassidy's sister, Katelyn, knew what she was doing when she escaped the clutches of Mama Sterling.*

I wanted to hurl my phone across the room. There was little love between my mother and me, and I'd often questioned whose interests she was really looking out for, but that did not mean I wanted our family drama dissected by soul-sucking reporters.

I had escaped. I couldn't help thinking that every time something like this appeared in the media. But Kassidy hadn't.

Nonsense. She'd made a different choice. That didn't make her a victim in this scenario. But still, guilt filled me as I looked over the pictures of Kassidy again. Those who didn't know her probably thought she was a starlet on the path to self-destruction, like Lindsey Lohan or Britney Spears circa the head-shaving incident. But that wasn't the case. Kassidy was fine. Sure, she partied too hard sometimes, but she was no different than any other twenty-one-year-old. Hell, I'd seen some similar occurrences in downtown Bleaksburg.

It's not the same. And I didn't really know if Kassidy was fine. I couldn't remember the last time I'd had a deep conversation with her. Maybe she really was struggling. While my mother could help Kassidy's career, she was clueless when it came to my sister's emotional well-being. *Clueless or careless?* I didn't want to examine that too closely.

The time difference between Virginia and California meant it wasn't quite dinnertime there. Taking several deep breaths, I dialed my sister.

"Hello?" she slurred.

Jesus, is she drunk?

"Kassidy, it's Katie."

"I know. That's why I answered." Her voice was clearer now.

"What are you doing?"

"I *was* napping."

Kassidy was like a grizzly bear being woken from hibernation when she first got up. This wasn't the best of circumstances to break the news. I swallowed. "I saw something online you should know about."

"Hmm?" There was a gulping sound on the other end of the line. She must be drinking something. Hopefully it was water. *Stop it. She's not drunk.* I couldn't get that idea out of my head.

"There are some pictures online, Kassidy."

"With Tate and the Corvette?" She finally sounded alert. "I know."

I paused, not expecting that reaction. I'd braced myself for hysterics, but instead I was greeted with eerie calm. "Is everything okay?" I asked gently.

"Not really. Those pictures aren't getting nearly the mileage they should."

I blinked. "Excuse me?"

She laughed. "You didn't think those were real, did you? They're a publicity stunt. I wasn't about to do a sex tape, and this was the next best thing."

"Are you kidding me?" I couldn't stop from yelling. How could she possibly think those pictures were *not* real?

That was *really* her crotch on display. And while the lipstick on Tate's pants might not mean she had been blowing him in the car, everyone would come to that conclusion. The incident would stain her reputation forever.

"Don't be so uptight."

"Kassidy, a picture of you flashing your vag is online." I wanted to continue, but if she didn't already understand why that was a problem, I wouldn't be able to explain it to her.

"Are you worried because we're identical?" She giggled. "So it's like your vag has been exposed too?"

We'd stopped being identical once Kassidy had started tinkering with plastic surgery. We'd always been different personality-wise, but I'd always been able to relate to her. She was my twin—I thought that meant I would know her no matter what. I was wrong.

My fingers tightened on my phone. "I was just concerned for you, but I see now it was unwarranted. Have a nice night, Kass." I hung up and powered down the phone. I had no idea if she would call me back, but I was done talking to her.

CHAPTER 9

Wyatt

"YOU WANT THREE or four eggs?" I started cracking eggs into a bowl.

Behind me, Angie snorted. "Two."

I grinned. "Right." I couldn't remember the last time I cooked for someone other than me or Freddie. I'd forgotten that normal people didn't eat a half dozen eggs every morning for breakfast.

"Ugh!" Angie muttered. "Another freaking typo." Her printer was on the fritz—again—so she'd called me a half hour ago asking to come over and use mine before she had to meet up with her study group. At the moment, she was poring over her part of their project.

"You could try changing the font," I suggested. "Then it'll look different on the screen."

"Nope. Tried that. The only thing that works for me is reading it over on paper." Her voice was laced with frustration. Angie was smart, and sometimes her brain moved faster than her eyes could keep up, which led to missing words and typos.

Toast popped up in the toaster. I plucked it out and set it on a plate. "Jelly?" I put the plate in front of Angela.

She shoved her papers to the side and pushed her dark, curly hair out of her face. "Just butter, thanks."

I fished it out of the fridge for her and turned back to the stove. When my phone rang, I slipped in earbuds and tucked the phone in the waistband of my sweatpants.

"What's up?" I asked as greeting to Freddie. Besides my grandparents, he was the only one who ever called me. Most people just texted.

"I'm feeling antsy. I know it's our rest day, but do you want to go for a run?"

I looked out the window at the snow covering the ground. "I'm not looking to go all *Rocky IV* today."

"Man, you're a slacker. What you up to anyway?"

I dumped a mountain of eggs on one plate and a tiny amount in comparison on the second. "Making breakfast for a smoking-hot female." I winked at Angie as I set the plate in front of her. She rolled her eyes.

"What?" Freddie's voice rose an octave. "You brought that girl home?"

"What do you think?" If I had brought Katie home, I wouldn't be on the phone with Freddie. Not wanting to embarrass myself with a massive hard-on in front of Angie, I forced myself not to think about what I might be doing if I was with Katie right now.

I never brought girls home. My address wasn't a secret, but I didn't advertise it either. Besides that, I hadn't yet figured out a way to tactfully kick a girl out when it was time for her to go. It was easier to go to her place so I could leave.

"Oh, is Angie's printer acting up again?" Freddie sighed. "I told her to throw that damn thing off the balcony."

"She's not going to do that," I replied. "Then she'd have no excuse to come see her favorite guy."

Freddie laughed. "You trippin'."

"When is the last time *you* made her breakfast?"

There was a pause. "Now you're making me look bad. I see how it is."

I laughed. "I'll call you later." I yanked the earbuds out of my ears and tossed them, along with the phone, onto the counter.

Angie's lips were pursed as she stared at me. "Why did you have to go and do that? Now Freddie might actually try to cook for me." She shuddered.

I chuckled. I wasn't a gourmet chef, but I could get by. Freddie, on the other hand, could barely make a sandwich without screwing something up.

Taking a seat next to Angie, I nudged her. "Do you want me to look over that before you go?" She was damn near obsessive when it came to making sure there were no mistakes in her work before she met with her group. I still remembered the great sophomore-year tragedy of her notes containing *to* instead of *too*.

She pushed some eggs onto her toast with her fork. "Thanks, sweetie, but I gotta print out a fresh copy and get going as soon as I'm done eating. What did Freddie want?"

"What else? To work out."

She sighed. "That boy is beyond stressed."

"Can you blame him?"

"Not really, but he's got to understand there are other things happening in life besides the damn combines. I had to kick him out of my place last night because he wouldn't settle down, and I couldn't concentrate with him there. I've got shit to do, too, you know?" She paused. "He wants me to quit school."

I blinked. "Really?" Angie was a straight-A student, and while she still had no clue what she wanted to do with her degree, I had no doubt she would be awesome wherever she ended up. Besides that, she wasn't a quitter. It went against who she was.

"Yeah, so that might have been part of the reason I kicked him out. I was trying to work on my part of this project, and he kept telling me to blow it off because he's going to take care of me anyway."

I grimaced. Sometimes I wondered how Freddie could be so blind when it came to his girlfriend. It was like he didn't even know her.

Angie noticed my reaction and nodded. "*Exactly*. I had to work my ass off in high school to make the grades to get into this school, and I've continued to work my ass off to keep my grades up."

I playfully leaned back to take a look at her ass. "I don't know. You've still got quite an ass."

She swatted me. "I'm serious, Wyatt. I told him I'm willing to put off grad school, but I'm not dropping out."

"Grad school?"

"Yeah." She fidgeted. "I like school. I was thinking I might want to work at a university, in administration or something. I'd need an advanced degree for that."

That wasn't the kind of career that was easily transient, like working as a nurse or a teacher. It was the type of job where she would have to go where the job was, kind of like football. What were the odds that Freddie would play in a city where Angie could have the career she wanted? It wasn't impossible, but definitely unlikely.

Angie was looking at me expectantly.

"I... I don't know what to say."

"Yeah, I know." She sighed. She'd been with Freddie since the beginning, so she knew the demands of football almost as well as we did. "He could have played for Alabama or Ohio, but he chose here because of me."

I knew Freddie had had offers from several big football programs, but I hadn't realized Angie had factored so much into his decision. He was from Hampton, so I'd figured he had wanted to stay in state and close to family.

"That wasn't much of a sacrifice," I assured her. "Don't forget we just won a national championship."

"I know, and I didn't ask him to make that decision. But now he's looking at me to make a sacrifice, and I don't know if I can do it. I love him." Her big brown eyes glistened with tears. "But I can't do something that would make me resent him. That's not good for either of us."

I exhaled. Angie was one of the most levelheaded people I knew. She had to be to put up with Freddie's shenanigans. Most stuff rolled off her back, but the fact that she was talking about the situation meant it was serious.

"It's only one year, right? Surely you can make it work."

"We've never been apart, not since we were fifteen. Sometimes I wish Freddie was like you, sticking it out for the full four. But that's not the right decision for him. He can't hack it academically."

"I'm sorry. I don't know what to say," I said again. I'd always looked at Freddie and Angela as being the one couple who'd gotten it right, but I supposed that was naive. The life he and I had chosen had the potential to be very lucrative, but it came with a shit ton of complications.

Wiping her eyes, Angela laughed. "You don't have to say anything. I'm sorry to unload on you like this, but it feels damn good to get it out."

"Of course," I said. "Anytime."

She pushed her plate aside and opened her laptop. "I'd offer to do the dishes, but that would make me late."

I stood and cleared both of our dishes. "Don't worry about it." I paused, feeling like I was about to betray my best friend. Bro code should dictate that I was on Freddie's side no matter what. But I couldn't bear to see Angela hurting. She hadn't just been a constant in Freddie's life—she'd also been a constant in mine. And for the first time, I realized how much I would miss her if she weren't there next year, or hell, how much I would miss her when we went our separate ways after graduation.

I cleared my throat. "Angie, you've got to do what's right for you. If Freddie doesn't realize that you're worth waiting for for one year, he doesn't deserve you. Deep down, he wants what's best for you. He's just scared."

"I know. So much change is scary. But I'm not going anywhere, literally and figuratively." She laughed. "Now, not to be rude, but leave me be so I can finish this."

I ducked my head, properly admonished. "Yes, ma'am."

* * *

Katie

PRINCESS BUTTERCUP WAS sitting on my head. *On. My. Head.* With eyes still closed, I reached up to gently nudge her aside when what I really wanted was to shove her off the bed entirely. But lurking inside those cute furry paws were razor-sharp claws, and I didn't want to lose an eye.

When she'd settled herself on my pillow instead of my head, I glared at her. "Why don't you bother your owner like this? You're Rachel's cat, not mine."

The feline's tail twitched as if to say *eff you too, bitch.* She didn't move.

I glanced at my alarm clock, which read 11:17. Shit, it was late. After I'd gotten off the phone with Kassidy last night, I'd gone to bed immediately, but of course I'd tossed and turned before falling into a restless sleep.

Wyatt had wanted me to dream about him, and I had, but probably not in the way he'd intended. Or if he had intended the types of dreams I'd had, he was one sick psycho.

I'd dreamt that Wyatt had taken me to see the new billboard advertising the football team, except when we got there, it was a giant picture of me getting out of the Corvette, displaying my womanly bits to the world.

I was so pissed at Kassidy. She wanted to shed her child star image, but hadn't her role on *Cali Girls* already done that?

The major difference between Kassidy and me was that she loved the fame more than the acting itself, whereas I was the opposite. Perhaps she didn't care about being a respected actress as long as she was getting the attention she desired. I didn't understand it.

I wondered if the stunt had been her idea or our mom's. I hated that I had to consider that, but the article wasn't completely wrong about "Mama Sterling."

Sighing, I turned on my phone to see if I had a missed call from Kassidy. *Nope.* I guessed my concern meant nothing to her. I shouldn't have been surprised. Though we'd shared a womb at one point, we'd shared little since I'd left the biz. Even before then, my anxiety over the fame and her need for more of it had driven a wedge between us.

Princess Buttercup randomly started purring, so I pulled her to me, tucked her under the covers, and scratched her ears how she liked. "Maybe you're not all bad," I muttered.

I wondered if Wyatt was a cat person. Somehow, I couldn't picture him tucking a cat into bed next to him. But tucking me in? Oh, yes, I could—

Just stop right there.

I could admit it—I had the hots for Wyatt Archer, but more than that, I liked him as a person. None of that mattered, though. Last night after our date, I'd been toying with the idea of seeing him again, but I was going to take my dream for what it was—a warning. There was a reason my subconscious had involved Wyatt in my biggest fear.

The second Princess Buttercup stopped purring, I dragged my ass out of bed before the bipolar feline took a nip out of my face. After throwing a load of laundry into the machine, I got in the shower and stayed there until the water ran cold, which wasn't terribly long. *Damn it.* I'd already called management about our hot water heater once, but apparently they needed a reminder. Though they shouldn't. The thing went wonky every other week.

Wrapped in a towel, I padded back to my room to find Rachel wearing rubber gloves with my phone pressed to her ear. *What the hell?*

She grinned deviously when she saw me. "Here she is." Before handing over the phone, she hit the speaker button.

I glanced at it. *Damn it.* It was Wyatt.

What the fuck? I mouthed. She shrugged and stayed put. Why had she been talking to him on *my* phone? And what the hell could she have said to him? *Oh God.*

She manically gestured to the phone.

"Hello?" I asked tentatively.

"Hey, how'd you sleep?" His voice was low and smooth, and it sent heat to my nether regions.

I turned my back to Rachel and prepared to turn off the speaker when she grabbed my arm to stop me. My towel slipped, and I clutched at it with one hand while Rachel firmly held my other arm so I couldn't turn off the speaker.

Oh no, she isn't. And she had been threatening to revoke my BFF card?

"You still there?" Wyatt asked.

I cringed. "Yeah, sorry. I slept well. You?" God, this was awkward. It would have been even without Rachel listening in. It felt like the morning-after conversation, except we hadn't even spent the night together.

He paused, making me wonder if he was concocting some BS line about how his bed was lonely or something. Though with his reputation as a ladies' man, he probably had cheesy lines like those at the ready. Hell, he was the

Archer. He could sing the alphabet song off-key, and girls would still drop their panties at his feet. *Me included.*

"Good. Do you want to go snow tubing?"

"What?" I'd half-expected him to be calling to tell me something had fallen out of my purse in his car last night. I certainly hadn't expected the Archer to be asking for a second date less than twenty-four hours after our first one, especially since I couldn't figure out why he'd left so abruptly the night before.

"Yeah. I know it's last minute, but Freddie, Angie, and I are going in a few hours, and I thought you might want to go." He cleared his throat. "I was *hoping* you'd want to go."

Beside me, Rachel's mouth opened into a silent scream, and she hopped up and down. I glared at her and put a finger to my lips, not an easy feat without dropping my towel or the phone.

"I don't know," I hedged.

"There'll be hot chocolate. Don't forget you gave me a rain check for dessert."

"I'm not a big fan of snow." But I *was* a big fan of Wyatt. As was every other football-loving VVU fan. God, why couldn't our circumstances be different?

"I'll keep you warm," he said. And there it was—the lame pick-up line. Even though I could identify it as such, my insides melted.

In the background, I heard a girl speaking. "Stop with those lame lines, Wyatt. Let me talk to her."

"Hang on," Wyatt said.

"Hey, girl, it's Angie, Freddie's girlfriend."

"Hi." I was too stunned to say anything else.

"So my man, Freddie, is a big pansy and is afraid of snow tubing."

"It's a serious fear!" he shouted in the background. *"I could break something!"*

"Hush up," Angie told him. "But Wyatt and I really want to go. If you go, Freddie will too. So do a girl a solid and come with us."

My brain was taking too long to process everything that was happening. "I don't know…"

"You and Freddie can tube once, and if you don't like it, then you can hang out inside like a wimp. Not you, Katie, but Freddie. Freddie is the wimp. You'd just be keeping the wimp company."

I couldn't stop my burst of laughter. But as amusing as Angie was, I had decided that pursuing things with Wyatt would be bad. "I don't think I have the right clothes. I don't have a snowsuit or anything like that."

"She can borrow mine!" Rachel blurted loudly.

"Is that Rachel?" Wyatt asked. *Great.* It sounded like they were on speaker too. This had turned into a regular conference call. And exactly how long had Rachel been talking to him before I came into the room anyway?

"Yup. Katie's BFF at your service."

I eyed her as she said that last part, and she eyed me right back, as if daring me to take away her status. She had no clue how close I was to letting Princess Buttercup take her place.

"Do you want to come too?" Wyatt asked, and my heart warmed at his immediate willingness to include my friend.

"I already have plans," Rachel said, "but thanks for asking."

It was thoughtful of him to ask and made me wonder if I was jumping the gun by thinking this was a double date. Maybe it was only a group outing that happened to have two girls and two guys.

Snort. Even my brain couldn't sell itself on that logic.

"Is anyone else going?" I asked.

"Nope, just the four of us," Wyatt said. *So definitely a double date.* "Can you be ready at two?"

I glanced at the clock. That left me a little over an hour. "Sure," I found myself saying.

"Great. See you soon." Wyatt disconnected.

I whirled on Rachel. "What in the ever-loving hell?"

Something in my expression must have scared her—and rightly so since I was pissed—because she put up her yellow-gloved hands. "Your phone rang, and I saw it was him, so I answered it. You'd just gotten out of the shower, and I didn't want you to miss the call."

"It would be no big deal to miss the call," I said angrily.

She shook her head. "I know you. You'd hem and haw about calling him back, and I saved you from that."

"You didn't *save* me from anything. You helped bully me into going snow tubing."

"*Bully you?* Seriously?" She threw her hands up. "You like him. I know you do. Give me one good reason you shouldn't go out with him again. And don't say because he's the Archer." She made air quotes with her gloved fingers when she said "the Archer."

I looked down at the carpet. I couldn't explain it to her because she didn't know about my past. "It won't work out."

Right then would have been the perfect time to clue her in. She'd been my best friend for three years, and I knew she would never betray the confidence. But still, I held back because the conversation deserved more than the few minutes I had to spend on it.

"I'm not saying it has to," she said. "Just go hang out and have some fun. If it works out, great. If not, then at least you won't wonder what could have been."

"I wouldn't wonder," I muttered, knowing the words were a flat-out lie.

She squeezed my hand. "Look, if it turns out this was a mistake, I apologize in advance. But you deserve to have some fun. It feels like yesterday that we were moving into the dorms, and now we're juniors. College isn't going to last forever."

I eyed Rachel suspiciously. Since when had she gotten all philosophical and shit? But she had a point.

"Okay." I exhaled. "I forgive you."

She snorted. "I wasn't asking for forgiveness."

I shot her a dirty look, and she put her hands up again. I frowned at the yellow gloves. "What's up with those?"

She tucked them behind her back. "Uh, yeah. Princess Buttercup hocked up a hairball on your bed, and I was trying to get it cleaned up before you found out. That's why I was in here and heard your phone."

I put a hand over my eyes. "Please tell me it wasn't on my pillow."

"Okay. I won't."

CHAPTER 10

Wyatt

FREDDIE BITCHED AND moaned the entire drive to Katie's apartment. Angela sat in the back seat, tapping her fingers on her knee to the beat of the song on the radio. She'd perfected the art of tuning him out, but I hadn't.

"You're not going to break your neck," I told Freddie for the forty-seventh time. "At worst, you'll fall out of the tube and look like an idiot."

He paused and stared at me with his mouth slightly ajar. "And that's supposed to make me feel better?"

"How is it we've been up here for three years and we've never gone tubing or skiing or anything?" I asked, slightly changing the subject. I couldn't handle playing nursemaid to Freddie anymore. "It's only an hour away."

"Some of us have the sense not to risk harm to our bodies." Freddie gestured to his legs. "Do you know how much these legs are worth?"

My fingers tightened on the steering wheel. "I guess we'll find out soon," I muttered.

Angela and I had come up with the idea to go tubing to distract Freddie. I had also hoped it would take my mind off things for a while. But we weren't even en route to Snow Scene, and the draft had already crept back into the conversation. It was inevitable, and I couldn't blame Freddie. The biggest thing to ever happen to him was mere weeks away. Of course it was going to come up.

I parked in the same visitor's spot as the night before. "Be right back." I hopped out of the car and trotted to Katie's building.

Freddie had only agreed to go if I brought a date, with the stipulation that one of Angela's friends didn't count. He had been using it as an out, but the joke was on him. Normally, I would've played it cool and not called Katie so soon. Hell, my "normal" would be not to call the girl at all. Everything about Katie had me throwing norms out the window. I scrubbed a hand over my face as I took the stairs two at a time.

What the hell am I doing? My talk with Angela that morning had made me realize that dating a player required sacrifices on the girl's part too. I'd never thought about it from that angle because usually the girls I attracted were ones who wanted to exploit my status. So as with everything else in my life these days, I couldn't help but question if I was making a mistake pursuing Katie.

Katie opened the door after my first knock. The sight of her answered my question. I was not making a mistake. She wore all black—tight-fitting Lycra that showed her every curve. My gaze traveled her body down to her toes and back up again to land on her face. Her cheeks were tinged pink, probably from embarrassment because of how blatantly I'd checked her out. But her eyes met mine, as if to hold her ground despite my ogling. My grandpa's words filled my head, and I felt like an ass. But damn... she should have warned me. I wasn't the violent or possessive type, but if any other guy looked at her the way I just had, I might be tempted to crack his skull.

"You ready?" I asked, carefully keeping my gaze on her face.

She nodded and stepped over to the couch to gather her things. Remembering the escape-artist cat, I came in and shut the door behind me.

She turned, clutching a dark-purple ski suit to her chest. "Do I need anything else?"

I shook my head. "It's basically like sledding on an inner tube from what I understand. I've actually never been. None of us have."

"I grew up in Florida, so I'm not used to the snow." She gestured to the door, and I took her cue.

"What brought you to Virginia, then?" I asked as she locked the door.

"My grandfather went here. My grandparents were older and died a few years ago, but my memories of them are filled with VVU memorabilia."

As we approached the car, Freddie hopped out and climbed into the back next to Angela. I held the passenger door for Katie then got back in the driver's seat. I twisted in my seat to make the introductions. "This is Angela."

"And you're Katie." Angie held out her hand. "I'm so happy to meet you." The sugary tone of her voice alerted me to the fact that putting Angela with Katie might not have been a good idea. Angela had met some of the girls I'd spent time with, but only in passing at bars or parties. Katie would be lucky to escape the events of the afternoon without an interrogation.

As Katie shook Angela's hand, I nodded at Freddie, who was sitting behind Katie. "You probably already know Freddie."

Katie took one look at him crammed in the back seat with his knees practically hitting the roof of the car and burst out laughing. She clapped a hand over her mouth. "Sorry! That was rude. You look very uncomfortable. I don't mind sitting in the back if you need the legroom up here."

Freddie bobbed his head up and down. "I like this one, Archer. She's thoughtful, *and* she has the sense to stay out of the snow. Or at least until you talked her into it."

I snorted. "You were the one who wanted to go for a run outside."

"On the sidewalk that had been cleared of snow and covered in salt! I didn't want to roll around in it."

"Don't fall off your tube, and you won't roll around in it," Angela snapped. "Stop being a baby."

Freddie clucked his tongue. "You see how they abuse me, Katie? They're always ganging up on me. But now that you're here, that can end. Right, girl? You're on my side."

"I'll have your back if you have mine." Katie grinned. "I'm pretty sure I can put Wyatt in his place."

"You know," Freddie said, "I would very much like to see that."

I turned up the radio and threw the car in reverse before the conversation could get any further. *Oh yeah.* Bringing Katie out with these two definitely put me on dangerous ground.

* * *

Katie

THOUGH I DIDN'T participate much in the banter on the drive into the West Virginia mountains, I appreciated it. I saw a whole new side to Wyatt. And Freddie for that matter. To the world, they were the Archer and FM4, but in this small group, they were fair game for ribbing and verbal smackdowns. Angela didn't take shit from either of them, and I loved her for it.

I kept an eye on the car's temperature display, and the closer we got to Snow Scene, the colder it got. Though the temperature in the car had stayed consistent, I involuntarily shivered. I hadn't been lying when I told Wyatt I wasn't a fan of snow. I wasn't a fan of cold in general, but I'd wanted to get out of Florida, where my dad and I had moved to be close to my grandparents after I'd quit acting. The only thing I missed about Florida was its mild winter weather.

We weren't the only ones wanting to play in the snow. The parking lot was packed. When Wyatt finally found a space and we spilled out of the car, Freddie grimaced and stretched his legs. As he squatted and twisted, he groaned a little.

I immediately felt bad. "You could have sat in the front," I reminded him.

He grinned and plucked my nose. "Nah, girl. I'm just messing with you."

Angie rolled her eyes. "Cut the girl a break, Freddie. You're going to scare her off." She linked her arm through mine. "Come on. Let's find a place for you to put your snowsuit on, and the guys can get our tickets."

As she tugged me away, I glanced over my shoulder at Wyatt. His thumbs were hooked in his pockets, and the left side of his mouth quirked up. He was watching me walk away and appreciating the view, just as he had when he'd come into my apartment. Though I hadn't worn the black Lycra for his benefit, I wasn't above being pleased that he liked it.

Too bad I was about to cover myself with a purple snowsuit and look like the girl from the Willy Wonka movie. Part of me didn't care, though. I was freezing.

"Did you bring a suit?" I asked Angie, noticing she wasn't carrying one.

"No." She scanned the signage, presumably looking for the locker room. "I don't have one, so I'm wearing about seven layers. Peeing is going to be a pain in the ass."

I chuckled. "I was lucky that my roommate had one I could borrow."

We found the locker room, and I quickly slipped into the suit. When we went back outside and didn't see the guys, Angie checked her phone. "They're in line."

I scanned the crowds of people and easily spotted them by the ticket window. They stood about a head taller than everyone else. Plus, Wyatt was the best-looking guy around. I watched as women, young and old, took notice of him. Even so, it didn't seem like anyone recognized him, which surprised me considering how close we were to the university. Maybe he was right—maybe his fame didn't extend off campus or to those who didn't follow college football. His image wasn't shoved in people's faces like mine and Kassidy's had been when we were on *Sisters Squared*. During the show's heyday, I would have been hard pressed to find someone who hadn't heard of us.

Angie and I took a seat on a bench, and despite having only just met, we huddled together for warmth.

"How long have you and Freddie been together?" I asked. I knew it was a long time, but I wanted to make conversation.

"Since we were fifteen, more or less."

"Wow." I thought back to what I was doing when I was fifteen. I'd been busy trying to blend in at a public high school. *Spoiler alert.* It hadn't worked. Academically, I was behind from only having been tutored on set, and socially, I was a walking disaster. I was desperate to fit in and be normal, but the other kids wouldn't let me. They were split down the middle between those who were in awe of me and those who bullied me. Years later, I realized the bullying was a result of their own insecurities, but even if I had known that then, it wouldn't have helped. I was homeschooled for my first two years of high school before I tried again at a different high school. That time, I let my hair return to its natural dark color and took care to separate Katie Sullivan from Katelyn Sterling. It had helped that some time had passed since *Sisters Squared* was on prime time.

"Tell me about it," Angie grumbled. Then she laughed. "I'm only kidding. It's a little weird to feel like an old married woman at the ripe age of twenty, but I can't imagine life without him. Even before we dated, he was always just there, you know?"

I murmured and nodded even though I didn't really know. Other than my relatives, there was no one in my life who had known me since I was a child.

"He's a big flirt," Angie continued, "but that's just who he is. He's never strayed." She paused. "Partially because he knows I'd slice up his balls, sauté them, and shove them down his throat. But mostly because I'm awesome." She grinned.

Laughing, I nodded. "You are awesome." It was true, and I didn't have a problem telling her that. She didn't strike me as the type of person who was in danger of a swollen ego.

"It's tough sometimes with football, and sometimes I feel like football is his wife and I'm only his mistress, but sports is in his blood. It's part of who he is. If he weren't playing football, it would be track or basketball. You might wonder why I'm telling you all this. It's because most people—especially girls—want to know what it's like dating FM4. I'm not going to lie. Some of the guys on the team are total assholes who think they're God's gift, but most of them, like Freddie and Wyatt, are good guys."

"Oh," I said. "Yeah, I guess people would be curious." Then realization dawned on me. "Wyatt and I aren't dating. I mean, I guess this is a date, our second date, but—"

Angie put her hands up. "I'm not judging. Wyatt's like a brother to me. I'm sure you know he has a reputation for getting around."

I nodded slowly. "Now I'm confused. Why are you telling me this?" She was Wyatt's friend, so it didn't make sense for her to tout his flaws to his date, especially after she'd just said he was a good guy.

"I just want to make sure you're not going to hold that against him."

I didn't quite know how to respond. I definitely was holding something against him, but it was his fame, not his promiscuity. Though if I took some time to dwell on that, it would probably bother me more. Maybe it *should* have bothered me more, but the crazy Hollywood stories I'd heard from Kassidy had desensitized me to some of that. Though not enough to ignore my twin's vag pic.

"I'm here, aren't I?" I asked finally.

"You are, and it's shocking as hell. You should know that Wyatt has never brought a girl into his inner circle like this. It's not my place to speculate about what that means, but I thought you should know."

"Thanks." Her words left me perplexed. I'd known Wyatt had a reputation for getting around, but I hadn't known he'd kept that part of his life separate from his friends.

I watched as Wyatt and Freddie approached. Wyatt had a confidence in his walk—not a swagger, exactly, but a gait that said he knew exactly who he was. The confidence was sexy as hell. Even if he hadn't had the body of a god and a face too handsome for womankind's own good, his confidence would've been enough to make him attractive.

He held out a hand to help me stand, and when he pulled me to my feet, I was much closer to him than I'd anticipated. Heat filled my partially numb body, defrosting all my parts, and I suddenly felt suffocated by the snowsuit.

Wyatt took a step back so he could fasten my tubing pass to the zipper on my coat. I pulled off my gloves and reached up to help him. When my fingers brushed his, electricity zipped through my arms and exploded in my heart. *Oh boy.*

This moment was way too silent, way too intimate.

"I'll buy the hot chocolate later," I blurted out and immediately cringed. *Real smooth, Katie.* I'd planned to buy hot chocolate because it wasn't fair that Wyatt was paying for everything. Only I hadn't planned on announcing it so loudly.

Both Freddie and Angie looked over at us before returning to the task of affixing their tags. My cheeks heated, and I didn't even bother trying to figure out what they must be thinking.

"You got it," Wyatt said easily, either not noticing my awkwardness or politely ignoring it. He pulled a blue knit ski cap over his head and tugged on his gloves. "You ready?"

He took my hand and tugged me toward the bottom of the hill to get in line. For the first time ever, I was thankful for cold because the layers of clothing kept our skin from touching. The electricity that had shot through me when we touched before fried the circuits in my brain. I didn't trust myself to not do anything else stupid.

"Should we wait for Freddie and Angie?" I asked.

He looked back at where we'd left them and grinned. "We'll catch up with them later. Freddie is probably bitching and moaning about something. He's such a pansy."

I shoved my hands in my pockets and tucked my face down into the neck of my suit. It was freaking cold. I could only imagine how frigid it was going to be when the sun's weak rays were no longer providing slight warmth. Freddie wasn't the only pansy.

Wyatt nudged me. "You cold?" His posture was relaxed, and though his hands were in his pockets, there was no indication that he was bothered by the cold. He looked perfectly at ease.

"I'm okay." But my chattering teeth gave me away.

Wyatt grinned. "Come here."

I took a step closer, and he wrapped his arms around me, tucking my body against his. He briskly rubbed his hands up and down my arms. Heat spread to my limbs, chasing away the numbness that had taken hold. I nearly moaned. *So much for the layers stopping me from embarrassing myself.*

"Jesus," he said. "You're shivering."

"I'm from Florida," I reminded him. "Winters here kick my ass every year."

His response was to shift me to his side so he could unzip his jacket. Then he pulled me against his chest and wrapped his coat around me. All numbness left me in an instant, and my heart started hammering double time. Even through his layers of clothing, I could feel the hard lines of his body—taut pecs, tight abs, and powerful thighs. *Holy eff, he's cut.* I wanted to trace the lines of his body.

He looked down at me and grinned, giving me a perfect view of his perfectly straight white teeth. *He must have had braces.* There was no way such perfection could be natural.

"You're tiny," he said.

"Thanks?" I didn't know if that was supposed to be a compliment. Being wrapped up in him had made it hard to form coherent thoughts.

"I like it."

Right now, I liked *him. God help me.*

CHAPTER 11

Wyatt

KATIE STAYED TUCKED in my jacket while we rode the people mover to the top of the hill. The employee overseeing that area gave me a dirty look. He could fuck off. If it was a safety concern because of the conveyor belt beneath our feet, he could rest assured that I would never let Katie fall. She was safer with my arms around her than she would be anywhere else.

When I had caught sight of another guy checking her out while Freddie and I were buying the passes, it was all I could do to keep my cool. That wasn't like me. Despite the fact that some saw football as a violent sport, I wasn't a violent guy. Something about this girl brought out a protective streak in me. It wasn't that I saw her as weak— far from it. It was just that she had a vulnerability beneath the surface that became more evident to me the more time we spent together. *But hell, what do I know?* This was only our second date in less than twenty-four hours. I didn't really know her that well.

At the top of the hill, I was forced to release Katie so I could haul our tubes. I hadn't been cold before, but when she was no longer flush against me, a chill filled me. I liked her warm little body tucked into mine. As I arranged the tube at the top of the slope, I couldn't help but think I would much rather be sitting in front of a fire with Katie in my lap and wearing a lot fewer layers. She smiled at me as I held the tube for her to climb in, and I wondered if she would still be smiling if she knew what was going through my mind.

She looked up at me, her eyes filled with trepidation. *Huh. I guess Freddie isn't the only one who's scared.* But before I could ask her if she was okay, her tube launched down the hill. Grinning, I watched her dark hair fly out behind her and listened to her shriek. When I joined her at the bottom, she was laughing. Relief filled me, a strange reaction. But then again, Katie had told me she wasn't a fan of snow. I would feel like an ass for talking her into braving the cold if she ended up having a terrible time.

She pointed at the top of the slope. "Look. Freddie and Angie are about to go."

I turned and saw that Freddie only had a few people in front of him. Even from a distance, I could tell that my friend was nervous as hell. *Funny.* Two-hundred-and-fifty-pound linebackers crashing into him didn't faze him, but a tube and a bunch of snow did. When he got to the bottom, I was definitely going to point out the group of elementary-aged kids fearlessly hurtling down the slope.

I glanced at Katie. Her cheeks were tinged pink from the cold, and I wanted to unzip my jacket and pull her near me again. But damn, I hadn't been able to gauge her response last time, and I didn't want to freak her out.

I was in uncharted territory. I'd never had to question whether or not a girl I was with was into me. But if Katie wasn't feeling something between us, then why would she be there? Still, I couldn't shake the doubt that had begun to spread like a virus. It was uncomfortable, like a tourniquet was squeezing my lungs, making it hard to breathe.

What the hell, Archer? Snap out of it. I sucked in the frigid air and concentrated on the feeling of it filling my chest. Then I grinned at Katie and pulled her against me, forcing myself to act like I would with any other chick. Except with her body close to mine, it was evident that

Katie wasn't some random girl. She got under my skin, and I didn't know quite what to do about that.

Katie smiled up at me then turned her face toward the slope. "There he goes."

We watched as Freddie slid down the path, his hands gripping the tube tight. He yelped as the tube picked up speed.

Katie laughed. "I wouldn't have thought Freddie would be such a chicken."

"He puts on a good show, but he's a baby if he's out of his element," I said. "Angie probably made him go first to make sure he wouldn't back out."

She nodded. "Smart woman."

We only managed to get Freddie down the slope another few times before he hunkered down inside. The three of us didn't last much longer. Once the sun set, it was cold as balls out there. It didn't bother me since I was used to playing football in all types of weather, but Katie's teeth were chattering, and the tip of Angie's nose was bright red.

After Katie stripped off the snowsuit and was down to her black Lycra again—*fuck me*—we reconvened at a diner, where Freddie ordered half the menu.

"What?" he asked. "I didn't eat lunch."

Angela nodded to confirm. "He was too nervous about snow tubing."

Freddie let out an exasperated sound. "Woman, do you have to make me look like a fool in front of Archer's new girl?"

Angie shot him a bland stare. "You've got that covered on your own."

"Remind me again why I put up with you."

"Because I'm the best thing that's ever happened to you."

Nodding, Freddie looked at me and Katie. "She's right. I just need to be reminded every once in a while." He draped his arm casually over Angie's shoulder and pressed his lips to her temple. Their PDA was nothing new, but with Katie sitting next to me in the narrow booth, it was a different experience.

I want that.

I'd never cared before if a girl stuck around because I knew there would always be another one. They were interchangeable as far as I was concerned. I didn't care to know their favorite color or if they preferred strawberry or grape jelly. It was too much work, and for what? My mother had bailed on me and my father as soon as it had become clear the money was drying up. I didn't need or want the stress of wondering if a woman was with me for the right reasons. I was better off alone.

At least, I'd thought I was. But now I saw Freddie and Angie through a different lens. I'd always considered them an anomaly. What if they weren't?

Still, Angie and Freddie weren't without problems. That morning's conversation with Angie was proof of that. I was confident they would work it out, but they'd been together forever. Next year, I would be in the draft. Throwing the stress of a newer relationship on top of the normal stress of the draft would be stupid. Not to mention I would be MIA for most of the fall. Football had to come first, with my classes a close second. I wouldn't have time to be even a halfway decent boyfriend. It would be unfair to ask anyone to sign up for that.

As much as I was tired of it, staying single with the occasional hookup was the answer. Too bad Katie wasn't one-night-stand material.

* * *

Katie

I NOTICED THE instant Wyatt's demeanor changed—it was shortly after the server took our orders. He'd had his arm draped over the back of the booth, and he pulled it into himself and turned away. I didn't know what had caused the shift, whether it was the French toast I'd ordered for dinner or some other cause.

His moods changed more frequently than Princess Buttercup's. One minute he was zipping me up in his jacket, and the next he was giving me the cold shoulder. I didn't know what to make of it, and I didn't have the bandwidth to deal with it, so I ignored him in favor of chatting with Freddie and Angela.

I absolutely loved them. Freddie was a trip. To watch him play football, I would think he was some macho tough guy, but he was nothing but a big old softie. Angela was his perfect match, somehow tough and nurturing at the same time.

"Oh, I'm the best," he was saying. Despite being a softie and wrapped around Angie's finger, he was downright cocky. Somehow, though, it didn't put me off. It worked for him. "It's not a question of whether I'll go first round. It's a question of whether I'll go first, fifth, or tenth."

Angela gave me a look that indicated she'd heard his spiel before. "Sometimes I wonder how that ego fits in your long, skinny body."

"Come on, baby, you know I'm right. And I'll prove it to you when I buy you a mansion to live in."

"You're boring Katie. She doesn't care about this."

I shrugged. "It's interesting. I've never known a professional athlete."

Freddie's lips stretched into a Cheshire grin. "It'll be my pleasure to be your first." His eyebrows wagged suggestively.

Angie rolled her eyes, but beside me, Wyatt stiffened. "Don't be an ass."

"Chill, man. I'm just playing." Freddie locked his eyes on mine. "I'm just playing. I'm sorry if I offended you."

Eying Wyatt, I waved my hand dismissively. "It's all good. Besides," I said in a joking tone, "I don't need my honor defended."

Wyatt scrubbed a hand over his face. "Of course you don't. Sorry. I just..." He slid out of the booth and stood. "I'll be back in a minute." He walked toward the front door.

Shaking his head, Freddie stared after his friend. "I wish Wyatt had declared for the draft so he wouldn't be so damn moody."

"Maybe that's not it." Angie pointedly fixed her gaze on me. "Maybe it's something else."

I looked down at the table, not trusting myself to meet her gaze. "That's flattering, really, but we've only seen each other twice. I don't think I have that much pull over him."

"I don't know," Angie said. "He—*holy shit.* Is that... I think it is!" Her voice had taken on an odd whispering-scream quality.

Grateful for the reprieve, I scanned the diner to see what had gotten her excited.

"What are you looking at?" Freddie craned his neck.

"Don't stare!" Angie hissed, and I figured out who she was staring at. "I think it's Nathan Reeves."

Shit, shit, shit. She was right. I'd never met the man in person, but I would know him anywhere.

"Who's that?" Freddie asked, perplexed as to why his girlfriend was freaking out over a middle-aged white guy. Granted, he was more handsome than the average Joe. Actors generally were.

"He played Mr. Finch on *Cali Girls.*" Angie fanned herself, which was the reaction most girls in our age bracket had when they talked about Mr. Finch. He'd played a teacher on my sister's show and had turned into an unintended heartthrob. While the producers had no doubt planned for tweens to fawn over the show's leading teen characters, Mr. Finch had gained a cult-like following with both teens and their moms.

What were the effing odds that I would see someone from *Cali Girls* in the middle of Bumfuck, West Virginia? Exhaling slowly, I forced myself not to freak out. Kassidy and I no longer looked identical. There was no reason he would recognize me. Still, I rested my elbow on the table and covered my face with my hand.

Angie reached across the table and squeezed my free hand. "Come on," she said. "Let's go take a closer look."

I shook my head, not trusting myself to speak.

Angie gave up the pretense of not staring and craned her neck. "I've never seen a celebrity before."

"Girl, I'm about to be a celebrity," Freddie said.

Angie stared at him with pursed lips. "I'm not even going to dignify that with a response." She stood up. "Come with me."

Freddie sighed but slid out of the booth. "I can't believe I'm going with you to check out another dude. He's, like, old and shit."

"Hush up." Angie looked at me. "Last chance. Who knows when you'll get the chance to see a celebrity up close again?"

Every day in the mirror. Though that wasn't true anymore. I was no longer a celebrity. I was officially a has-been, and I was one hundred percent okay with that.

Well, maybe ninety-nine percent. Every once in a while, I would see a movie with a fantastic role and wonder what it would have been like to play the character.

"You go," I said in a shaky voice. "I'll stay here and watch our stuff."

Angie scuttled off with Freddie in tow. I risked a peek at Nathan. The years had been kind to him. His dark hair was still full and thick, and his frame looked solid, like he continued to take care of himself. Even though the writers had killed off Mr. Finch in the second half of the show, he remained one of the most popular supporting characters. To the best of my knowledge, Nathan hadn't found the same level of success with any other roles. If he had, he wouldn't be in a diner in the mountains of West Virginia, picking up a takeout order.

Giving him the eye, Angie circled him. The sight made my stomach churn. That could easily be me just trying to go about my life but having a face so recognizable that people gawked. I'd been lucky to get out when I had, while I still had growing and changing to do. I was a far cry from the girl who'd starred on *Sisters Squared*. As much as I hated to say it, Kassidy had done me a favor by getting her face tweaked. If we'd stayed identical, I would have been as easily recognizable as she was.

I was so intently watching Angie and Nathan Reeves that I didn't notice Wyatt had come back until he slid into the booth next to me.

"Sorry." He sounded much better. Taking a walk, or whatever the hell he'd done, had improved his mood.

"Still have a lot on your mind?" I asked lightly, remembering our conversation from the previous night. I couldn't believe only twenty-four hours had passed. It already seemed like so long ago.

"Something like that." He picked up his glass of water and inclined his head toward Angie. "What is she doing? I mean, I can *see* what she's doing, but why is she stalking that dude?"

Freddie was nowhere in sight, and Angie was indeed acting like a creeper. I sighed. She'd lost a shit ton of cool points for this behavior. Celebrities could make even the most levelheaded people act stupid.

"He's Nathan Reeves." When Wyatt looked at me blankly, I continued. "He's an actor who was on *Cali Girls*."

I could tell Wyatt was struggling to place the reference. "Is that the show about the rich, spoiled high school girls in California?"

Though the show was deeper than that, that was an apt surface-level description. I nodded.

Wyatt shrugged. "I never watched it. What the hell is he doing in West Virginia?"

"Beats me," I said. "Maybe he's from here." People often forgot that actors were not born and bred in California, even if that was where they ended up for work.

"Ohmigod." Angie collapsed into the spot across from me. "That man is hot."

Eying her, Freddie sat. "He's short."

I chuckled. Many celebrities—males in particular—were a lot smaller in real life than the screen made them appear. *Hollywood magic at its best.*

"Did you get an autograph?" Wyatt asked.

Angie shook her head. "I didn't want to bother him."

"Then how are you sure it was him?" Wyatt asked in a teasing voice. "He could have been the guy's doppelganger."

Angie shrugged. "As far as I'm concerned, that was Nathan Reeves. I can cross celebrity sighting off my bucket list."

"Was that seriously on your list?" Freddie asked. "Because if I get picked up by LA, you can spy on all the celebrities buying their groceries."

"They probably don't go shopping for their own groceries," Angie told him. "They have *people* for that." She turned to me. "Did you watch *Cali Girls*? I loved that show. It was the best."

"Yes." I watched *everything* my sister was in. Despite the fact that her career had the potential to negatively affect my life, I was proud of all she'd accomplished. Making it in Hollywood wasn't easy, but besides that, she'd turned into a damn good actress.

But sometimes that wasn't enough. My thoughts turned to Kassidy's most recent attention-grabbing stunt. I'd yet to process how she ever could have thought that was a good idea.

"I wish they hadn't canceled it," Angie was saying. "They could have followed the girls to college or something." She looked at me expectantly, and I made a noncommittal noise. I *really* didn't want to talk about the show, but I didn't know how to change the subject without being rude.

Luckily, our food arrived, and I was spared having to pretend interest in the one topic I avoided at all costs. Up until the past week, Kassidy and her show hadn't come up in conversation at all. I supposed I should be lucky the reminiscing about teen TV shows hadn't led down the rabbit hole of childhood shows. *Sisters Squared* definitely would have come up, and it would've taken all the acting chops I had left to pretend I was participating in the conversation as a mere viewer and not the star of the stupid show.

Sometimes I wondered if I was making things more complicated than they needed to be. Sure, the paparazzi had been interested in me when I was on the show, but that was years ago. I was a has-been. No one cared about me anymore.

Yet, wasn't Nathan Reeves also a has-been? That hadn't stopped Angie from freaking out over him. Even if reporters and paparazzi left me alone, I didn't want to worry about fans of the show gawking at me while I was buying tampons or pumping gas.

While we waited for the server to bring the check, Wyatt grasped my hand, flipped it over, and traced each of my fingers, going from the palm to the tips and back again. It was a relatively innocent gesture, but the sensation shot from my fingers to my core, making me imagine Wyatt's fingers tracing every part of my body. It was the nonchalant way he did it—like there was nothing extraordinary about him touching me—that did me in.

He made me *want*, something that had not happened in a long time. When his skin brushed against mine, my worries about keeping my past hidden faded away. I didn't want to be held prisoner by my past. I wanted to live in the present and throw caution to the wind. Maybe I would end up on Wyatt's list of flings, quickly forgotten, but I was no longer convinced that would be a tragedy. Worse would be if I never took the leap and was left wondering.

CHAPTER 12

Wyatt

WHEN THE CHECK arrived, I reluctantly let go of Katie's hand, but she was faster than me and grabbed the check holder. I tried to take it from her, but she held it out of my reach, or so she thought. I easily could have taken it from her.

"I got it," she insisted. It wasn't worth fighting over, so I let her pay.

On the way back into town, Angie asked me to stop at Target, but she wouldn't tell me why. I let her and Freddie off at the door and parked. Katie and I waited in the car.

Without thinking about it, I reached for her hand and traced her fingertips. Her nails were perfectly shaped and covered with clear polish. Her skin was so damn smooth, her fingers long and graceful. I wondered if she played piano. If she didn't, she should. She had the hands for it.

Her breath hitched, causing me to look over at her. Her eyes were wide, and she looked shaken. "Why do you do that?" she whispered.

My instinct was to drop her hand, but I didn't. Instead, I studied her hand. *Why the hell did I do that?* The answer was simple—I wanted to touch her. I'd never been the affectionate sort, but she brought it out in me. She brought a lot of things out in me, like a newfound need to throw all my past dating rules out the window. *Don't get attached. Don't get serious. Don't get close.* Following those rules had kept things clean and simple, but I was starting to wonder if simple necessarily meant better.

I took a deep breath. "Does it bother you?"

"No...yes... I mean no." She sighed. "Apparently, I don't know what I mean."

"If it bothers you, I'll stop."

She swallowed. "Don't stop."

I lifted her hand to my mouth and kissed each fingertip, one by one. Her breathing stopped, and I looked at her, still not letting go of her hand. Her eyes were closed, and her head was pressed against the headrest.

Fuck. I almost lost my fucking shit right there. I was just kissing her fingers, so I could only imagine her reaction when I kissed the rest of her.

When...

Goddammit, I had no right to this girl. One taste of her wouldn't be enough, and she deserved so much more than I was able to give her. A relationship wasn't in my game plan, and Katie wasn't the one-night stand type.

So why am I still holding her hand?

The sound of the back door opening snapped me out of my thoughts. I released Katie's hand and ran mine over my face. *What the fuck am I doing? Stick to the rules.*

Angie had a gleeful expression as she and Freddie piled back into the car.

"Do I even want to know?" I asked. Though I was joking, I was grateful for the interruption. I'd let things get too intense for a moment, but I couldn't seem to stop myself.

I didn't *want* to stop myself. And that scared the shit out of me.

Angie retrieved her purchase from the plastic bag and shoved it under my nose. "Cards Against Humanity!" she said. "Our night isn't over yet."

I'd heard of the game, but I'd never played. In general, I wasn't big on party games. *And fuck.* There went my plan to do both me and Katie a favor by taking her home.

"You all know each other, so you'll know what cards to play. I'm at a disadvantage." Katie's lips formed into a pout, and I no longer gave a fuck what the game was. I would play it all night long if Katie wore that sexy expression. *Christ.* At that rate, my brain wouldn't have an ounce of blood left in it by the end of the night.

"It's all right, girl," Freddie said. "I've never played, so you've got experience on your side."

We went back to my apartment because Freddie's was a disaster and Angie's roommates were likely home. Living alone was one of my few splurges. As much as I loved Freddie like a brother, sometimes I needed to get away from all of the noise. Solitude was underrated.

I opened my liquor cabinet and frowned. There was a lot of Jack and Jim, but not much in the way of girly liquor. Angie came over from time to time, but I didn't usually entertain women at my place. My apartment was my sanctuary.

I glanced over at Katie sitting on my couch. Her presence there should have bothered me—it had only taken me bringing a girl to my place once for me to decide never to do it again—but I liked seeing her in my living room, liked watching her look around to take measure of the place. I wondered what she thought. It was pretty bare—no pictures on the walls or any other decorative shit. I favored functional and comfortable, with a big-ass TV, of course.

Angie ripped the plastic off the game and read the instructions.

"I thought you've played before," I said.

"It's been a while."

I looked at the clock. *Damn.* It was after ten, so the liquor store was closed. "I don't have much for drinks, but I could run to Kroger for wine or something."

Freddie slipped his jacket back on. "I got this one, man." He disappeared out the front door.

I threw a few bags of chips on the coffee table. I might not have much for drinks, but my food stores were always stocked.

I sat next to Katie on the couch, so close our knees touched. I was a fucking sadist. Because after we played a few rounds of this game, I would have to take her home. Yet while she was there, I wanted to be close to her. And as much as I repeated my rules in my head, they meant nothing when it came to her.

It only took Freddie fifteen minutes to come back with a bag full of fruity drinks, and Angie quickly explained the rules of the game. Thirty minutes later, Angie, Freddie, and I gaped at Katie, who was winning by a landslide.

"What?" She self-consciously brought her nearly full bottle to her lips, and I remembered she'd told me she wasn't a big drinker.

"I don't know whether to be impressed by your skills or scared of what's going on in your mind," Freddie said.

Katie shrugged. "What can I say? I like winning."

Her statement put a grin on my face. *God, I like this girl.*

Freddie chuckled. "Then you're in the right group."

Angie gathered the cards and put them on the bottom of the deck. "These two can turn folding laundry into a competitive sport."

"You say that like it's a bad thing," Freddie said.

Angie's laugh quickly transitioned into a yawn. "I hate to be lame and call it quits so soon after we started, but my second wind came and went. I'm exhausted." She packed up the game.

"Your place or mine tonight?" Freddie asked her.

"Yours." She stood and shrugged into her coat. "Hailey was talking about doing her hair tonight, so the place probably stinks of chemicals. Katie, it was fun, girl. Let's do it again."

Katie stood and quickly hugged Angie. After my friends left, I retrieved my keys from the hook by the door. I didn't want to take Katie home, but I didn't trust myself alone with her. I cared about her too much to turn her into one of my conquests. *What the hell kind of shit is that? So much for not getting attached.*

Jingling my keys in my hand, I turned toward her. "You ready to go?"

She hadn't moved from her spot standing in front of the couch. "No."

I silenced my keys. "Okay. We can wait if—"

"What if I don't go home tonight?" she rushed on. "What if I stay here with you?"

Yes, fuck yes, please.

I closed my eyes. Katie didn't know what she was saying. I wanted nothing more than to take her into my bedroom, but I couldn't promise anything beyond that. As much as I wanted to be with her, to peel the black Lycra off her body, I couldn't bear to see her face when she realized what I could offer wasn't enough.

When I opened my eyes, she was only inches away from me. With shaking hands, she took the keys and returned them to the hook. Then she brought my fingertip to her lips in an imitation of what I'd done earlier in the car.

"That's not a good idea." But I did nothing to stop her. "Katie, don't." My voice was strained. "This isn't going to end how you think it is."

She stopped kissing my finger long enough to look at me quizzically. "Exactly how do *you* think it's going to end?"

With my hands fisted in your hair while you scream my name.

"I'm not a nice guy," I said. "I don't date girls. I hook up with them."

When Katie flinched, it was like nails were being slammed into my chest, but she needed to hear the cold, hard truth. Somewhere along the line, I had given her false expectations, which was totally my fault. And now I needed to set the record straight. *For both of us.*

She released my hand and stared at me. I struggled not to squirm as she scrutinized me.

"You're wrong," she said finally. "The fact that you're telling me that shows you're wrong."

I wanted to be wrong. But I didn't trust myself, not with my track record.

I shook my head. "I'm not, I promise you." I paused. "I like you. That's why I'm saying it."

"So do you only hook up with girls you don't like?"

Her comment should have made me feel better because it made me sound like an asshole, but it didn't seem to deter her. I ran both hands over my head. "Damn it, Katie, I'm trying to do the right thing here. You're a good girl."

She looked at her feet with a little chuckle and shook her head. "I'm tired of being good." Taking hold of my shirt, she yanked me closer to her then covered my lips with hers. Her tongue assaulted mine, and as she moaned into my mouth, my cock strained against my pants.

Gripping her ass, I pulled her against me, and her small, perfect breasts pressed against my chest. *Fuck me.*

I quickly turned us around and pressed her against the door. Her leg climbed up my thigh, and I grabbed her under the knees and lifted her so our bodies were aligned. I moved my mouth to her throat and ground against her. A deep, throaty sound escaped her, and she dug her nails into my shoulder blades.

God. Instinct was driving me, but my one last working brain cell remembered that I didn't want to be an asshole, not with her. I pulled my mouth away from her throat long enough to whisper in her ear. "I can still take you home. All you have to do is say the word, and I'll stop. It'll fucking kill me, but I'll stop."

"Don't you dare."

* * *

Katie

WYATT'S BODY WAS amazing—hard, strong, and tight in all the right places, which was *everywhere*. And his mouth. *Good God.* He'd put it on every inch of exposed skin, but it wasn't enough. I wanted more.

My legs were wrapped around his waist, and he had me pinned against the door. As his tongue found the delicate spot behind my ear, I moaned and arched my back.

My fingers found the edge of his shirt, and I tugged it up, but I couldn't get it over his head. He slipped his arm between my back and the door to brace me, then he carried me into the bedroom. I was wrapped around him like a damn spider monkey, but I'd never felt sexier.

He laid me on the bed then pulled his shirt over his head and tossed it aside. *Holy fuck.* Feeling his muscles through his shirt hadn't prepared me for the sculpted magnificence of his chest. My own nipples tightened at the sight of his. I'd never found men's nipples particularly attractive before, but I'd never seen them on such tight pecs. My gaze traveled south to the ridges of his abs and the glorious V muscle that disappeared into the waist of his pants.

Gimme. As I reached for him, my eyes met his. A smirk graced his face, and I should have been embarrassed at the way I'd worked him over with my gaze, but his eyes were just as hungry.

He leaned over me, and my fingers splayed on his stomach before traveling up to caress his chest. I wrapped my arms around his neck and pulled him on top of me. His tongue stroked mine, and the next thing I knew, my shirt had joined his. He ran his hands down the length of my torso. "You're beautiful," he said reverently.

He pulled down the cup of my bra, freeing my left breast, then went to work on it with his mouth. Heat shot to my core, and I rocked my hips.

His response was to push my hips down to the bed. "You drive me wild," he said against my skin. He took his kisses lower, down to my navel, and tugged on the elastic waistband of my pants. When he slipped a hand under it, he let out a hiss, which made me remember I wasn't wearing underwear under the Lycra.

His fingers found my folds, and I nearly cried out at his touch. It had been too freaking long since anyone had touched me there, much less someone who affected me like Wyatt. I pressed my face into a pillow to muffle my moans.

"Let me hear you," he said. "Don't hold back."

I pushed down his pants and traced the line of his muscle with my fingertip. He inhaled sharply. I went lower, lower, lower, until *ohmigod*. He was big everywhere.

Wyatt stripped my pants off, turning them inside out in the process. As his tongue explored my mouth, his fingers explored me. He plunged one in, and my hips jerked against his hand, my core vibrating. Clutching the sheets, I moaned. His finger set a steady rhythm.

"It's too much," I breathed. "I can't..." He kissed away my protests, and moments later, I clung to him as my world exploded and left me panting.

CHAPTER 13

Wyatt

I TUCKED KATIE against my chest just as I had on the slope. Only this time, she didn't need my heat. Her body was warm and lax, and her heart raced.

Making her come had been more satisfying than any time I'd gotten off myself. Fuck, I'd nearly come when I felt her clench around my hand and heard her moan. I could live and die a happy man if all I did was touch her body for the rest of my life.

I kissed her temple and smoothed her hair off her forehead. She was a fucking vision. Her cheeks were flushed, and her expression was relaxed and satisfied. And her body... She was gorgeous. I hadn't even seen all of her yet since her bra was still partially on, but I didn't have to to know she was perfect.

Still, I couldn't resist the urge to get the full picture. Shifting her in my arms, I unclasped her bra and freed her breasts. I'd thought I was satisfied lying there with her, but now that she was completely naked, I wanted to touch her again. My gaze traveled down her long, lean body, and I realized she wasn't actually naked—she still had her socks on. Chuckling, I reached down to pull them off.

Her eyes opened wide. "What are you doing?"

"I want to see all of you."

"Even my toes?"

I nodded solemnly. "Even your toes." Unlike her fingernails, which had no color, her toenails were painted a pale blue. It shouldn't have excited me as much as it did.

Christ. Everything about this girl did me in.

Like now, she was rallying and trailing lazy kisses down my neck. She mumbled something that sounded like "you're like a god."

"What was that, sweetheart?" I asked.

Though I couldn't see her face, I knew she was blushing. "I didn't mean to say that out loud. My brain is not all together there."

"You're in good company," I said. "My brain has no blood left in it."

She propped herself up on her elbow, and her lips quirked into a sexy smile. "Maybe I can help you with that."

Her hand started at my collarbone and trailed down my chest, circling each nipple before descending to my stomach. Every muscle in my body was tense as her hand dipped beneath my waistband. My body jerked, and I growled as her hand wrapped around my cock. She stilled.

"Don't stop," I rasped out. She eased my pants over my hips and down my legs. I threw my head back and enjoyed the sensation of her stroking me until I couldn't take it anymore. I quickly flipped our positions so that she was under me. Her mouth yielded to mine as her hands gripped my hips. My cock was grazing her entrance, but I took care not to press too close since I wasn't yet wearing a condom.

I took one out of my drawer and quickly sheathed myself. Then I nestled between Katie's legs and rested my forehead on hers. "This okay?" I asked quietly, wanting to make sure before I changed things between us irrevocably. More than that, I felt like I was also asking the question of myself. It would be hard as hell, but I could still walk away from her. After this, though, I wouldn't be able to.

"Please."

That one word nearly broke me. I pushed inside her, forcing myself to go slow as her body tensed. When she relaxed, I started to move. She spread her legs even wider, and I went in even deeper. *Holy fuck.* She was tight, slick, and wet. She threw one leg around my waist and moaned something that sounded like my name.

Hell, I'd nearly forgotten my own name. The only semblance of a coherent thought in my head was how right this felt, how I wanted to stay inside this girl forever.

She started to throb around my cock, and her fingers dug into my back. When I felt her shudder beneath me, I buried my face in her neck and allowed myself to let go.

* * *

I WATCHED HER sleep. Of course, since she was lying on my arm, I didn't have a choice unless I wanted to wake her, which I didn't. She was wearing one of my T-shirts, which dwarfed her. The hem had ridden up, and one gorgeous ass cheek was hanging out. I was so tempted to trace the curve of it, but again, I didn't want to wake her.

How the hell did I end up here?

Katie's eyelashes fluttered, a sign that she would wake soon. Fuck, I hoped things wouldn't be weird between us. I didn't have any experience with the morning-after shit. I structured my life to keep things uncomplicated. This, by definition, was complicated.

I didn't have time to dwell on it because her eyes opened. She blinked a few times, and I could tell the second she remembered where she was. Wide-eyed, she looked at me. Our faces were only inches apart. Morning breath be damned, I placed a light kiss on her lips.

Stretching, she smiled. "Good morning."

I grinned. "It's a very good morning." And it was. *Fuck uncomplicated.* If waking up next to Katie with her hair tousled, her naked body hidden only by my T-shirt, and her lips swollen—especially knowing I was the reason for that—was complicated, then deal me in.

* * *

Katie

WYATT OFFERED TO lend me clothes, but it would have been more awkward coming home while trying to keep the much-too-large clothes from falling off my body than just wearing yesterday's outfit home. He pulled to a stop in front of my apartment building and put the car in park.

Slipping his hand under my hair and around the back of my neck, he pulled me in for a heart-hammering kiss. *Holy hell*, he was good at that. Angie's words from the night before flitted through my mind, but I shook them off. As long as he was using his skills to my benefit, I didn't care how he'd acquired them.

"Call me later," he said.

Barely able to remember my own name, I nodded dumbly. I hopped out, and the cold was a harsh slap in the face after being in his warm embrace. Climbing up the stairs to my apartment, I realized the cold air wasn't the only slap in the face—so was reality.

Shit. I'd spent the night in the Archer's bed. We'd only been on two dates, and the first one had been a mere thirty-six hours ago. I wouldn't classify that as us dating, and I'd already slept with him. I waited for feelings of regret to wash over me, but they didn't come. Last night had been toe-curlingly fantastic. And Wyatt had been so sweet that morning by cooking me breakfast before he had to meet with a trainer. I got the impression that he was out of his element and that his actions weren't normal. He might have earned the reputation of being a player, but his words and actions were genuine.

He likes me.

That was a doozy to wrap my head around. Even more so, I liked him back. It figured that I would fall for the most famous guy on campus.

Holding my breath, I unlocked the front door and stepped inside. Rachel was nowhere to be seen. *Whew.* I would follow the BFF code and give her all the juicy details eventually, and I promised Wyatt I would call him later, but I needed some time to myself first.

When I walked into my room, Princess Buttercup was sitting on my pillow. Even from the doorway, I could see the layer of shed fur she was leaving behind. She gave me the evil eye, as if to say, *that's what you get for abandoning me.*

I glared right back. "I don't owe you anything," I muttered. Yet I still found myself reaching for her to mollify her hurt feelings. She allowed me to scratch her ears for a moment before sauntering off.

I flopped onto my bed and hugged my stuffed blue unicorn to my chest. I hadn't planned to have almost my entire weekend taken up by Wyatt, so that meant I had to spend the afternoon studying for a genetics test and reading *Twelfth Night* for my Shakespeare class. I curled onto my side. What I really wanted was to take a nap. I hadn't gotten much sleep on my sleepover.

But instead, I dragged myself off the bed and headed to the shower. Even though I was wearing my own clothes, I still smelled like Wyatt, and I was strangely reluctant to wash off his scent.

Crazy. That was what all of this was. Even if I weren't worried about Wyatt's fame calling unwanted attention to me, he still wasn't the best boyfriend material. Next year, he would go into the draft, and I would be applying to med schools. If I had any chance of getting accepted, it was time to buckle down and not waste my weekends away. My workload was only going to get heavier, especially as I started prepping for the MCAT.

But Wyatt was plenty busy too. Sure, we'd spent a lot of time together this weekend, but I couldn't believe he would always have time for that. Later this spring, his football schedule would ramp up, and he also had to maintain his academics. So maybe I was looking at things the wrong way. Both of us would be pressed for time, which made each of us the perfect partner for something light and casual. Like Rachel had said, college wasn't going to last forever. I would have fun with Wyatt until it wasn't fun anymore.

I was doubtful he was looking for anything more than that anyway.

Though there had been nothing casual about the way he'd tucked my naked body against his or the way he'd worshiped me with his eyes, his hands, and his mouth.

Good God... The memory of it made me go hot all over. I only hoped the thought of us together was having the same effect on him.

CHAPTER 14

Katie

THE DOUBLE DS pounced on me as soon as they walked in the door Wednesday evening.

Destiny gripped my arms. "Tell. Me. Everything."

"Hello, Destiny," I said serenely. "It's nice to see you too." I wasn't trying to milk this... Okay, maybe I was a little bit. I was the tame one of the group, so I rarely had anything juicy to spill.

Danielle passed off a plate covered in plastic wrap to Rachel. "Let her go, Des. She's not going to hold out on us." She narrowed her eyes at me. "Are you?"

I laughed. "I'll tell you everything I told Rachel."

"She was stingy with the details!" Rachel called from the kitchen.

I rolled my eyes. What were they expecting? A *Fifty Shades*-style play-by-play? *Nope. Not happening.* That was reserved for my mind alone. Those memories could keep a girl warm at night for a long, long time.

"You can tell as much as you're comfortable with." Danielle grinned. "As long as that includes everything."

I gave her a sly look. "If I did that, I'd ruin you for all other men, and I'm not willing to share."

Danielle gasped. "Are you serious?"

Looking at her wide eyes, I laughed. "About the sharing? Yes." I was serious about the other part too, but I let that go unspoken. Wyatt was as skilled in the bedroom as he was on the football field.

After I gave them a recap, glossing over the more intimate parts, Destiny sighed. "Does he have any single friends?"

I shrugged. "Not sure. Freddie is spoken for."

"Even if I was the man-stealing type, I'd stay away from him." Destiny shuddered. "Angela scares me."

"She's cool," I said. "But you're right—she doesn't take any shit. Though if Freddie cheated on her, she'd go after him, not the girl. Not that he would ever do that."

"When do you see Wyatt again?" Danielle batted her eyelashes. "I might conveniently be here when he comes over."

"I'm not sure." But now that I knew her plan, I definitely wouldn't tell her. I thought she was joking, but the look she exchanged with Destiny made me wonder. If Wyatt was just a regular guy, they wouldn't be so interested in him, but because he was the Archer, their common sense had gone on hiatus. It was irritatingly reminiscent of how Angela had acted in the diner when she'd seen the actor from *Cali Girls*.

My and Wyatt's schedules had been crazy this week, so while we'd texted daily and chatted once, I hadn't seen him since he'd dropped me off Sunday morning, nor had we made weekend plans. *As it should be.* My heart jumped into my throat with every text, forcing me to remind myself that the only way things could work between us was if we kept it light. Even if it lasted, it would inevitably end at the end of next year.

Look at me. I'm practically naming our children. Talk about counting my chickens. I was assuming we would still be seeing each other beyond the end of the month. That was a big assumption. He could be tired of me by next week.

I hoped not. I had other things to stress about, like the practice MCAT test waiting for me. *Ugh.* That was yet another reason I should have stuck to my no-dating policy.

"What are we watching tonight?" Rachel asked, unscrewing the cap on a bottle of cheap wine.

"We stopped in the middle of the first season of *Cali Girls*," Danielle said. "But we don't have to finish it. We can move on to something else."

I should have felt relieved, but instead I felt indifferent. For some reason, avoiding Kassidy's show didn't seem as important as it had last week. Perhaps it was the fact that we'd watched several hours of it together and no one had pointed her finger at me and declared, "You're the long-lost child star Katelyn Sterling!" Or maybe I'd finally put things in perspective.

The notion that reporters and paparazzi were hiding in the shadows, waiting to unmask me, was ridiculous. The only time my name ever came up was in conjunction with Kassidy's, and even then, I was a footnote in her past. I was self-absorbed to think anyone cared about where I was and what I was doing. Celebrities more famous than me had disappeared from the limelight with no issues. It was time to stop letting my past dictate my present.

"Play it." My words came out more forcefully than I'd meant them to. I cleared my throat. "Let's finish what we started," I amended.

Taking the glass of wine Rachel offered, I settled in to watch a vision of what my life could have been like had I chosen a different path. It made me realize I felt pretty damn content with my current life.

* * *

Wyatt

I knocked on Coach Gurgin's front door and stuck my hands in my pockets. While he considered all the players "his boys," he also maintained a professional distance, which did not include inviting players to his house. So when he'd called that morning, I'd known something was up.

The door swung open, and the grizzled, legendary coach appeared, though his rough edges somehow looked smoother in his foyer than in the locker room. The man inspired fear in his players, but he also made his players want to perform better, to be more. He'd shaped VVU's program over the last two decades and turned it into a respected institution.

And now he was leaving. He didn't have to tell me—his expression said it for him.

"Wyatt, come in." He *never* called any of us by our first names. *Damn it.*

I stepped inside. "Thank you, sir." I followed him into the front room, which was nice and toasty thanks to the fire in the fireplace. I waited until he sat and gestured for me to join him.

"I'm sure you're wondering why I asked you to stop by."

"You're leaving," I blurted before I could stop the accusatory words.

His eyes were sad as he nodded. "The decision wasn't made lightly, even if it seems sudden. I figure I owe all my boys an explanation, but you most of all."

It was on the tip of my tongue to tell him he didn't owe me anything, but damn it, I'd declined going into the draft based partially on his advice. I hadn't only decided to stay with VVU—I'd decided to stay with *him.*

"Why?" I asked. "Why now?"

"Judy is sick."

It took a moment for the words to register. Judy was his wife, and now that he mentioned it, I hadn't seen her in a while. She was normally a fixture in the front row of the stadium at games, but she hadn't attended the last few. Hell, she'd even missed the championship. The signs were there, and if I'd paid attention, I would have seen them.

"What..." I trailed off, realizing that the specifics were none of my business. "Will she be okay?"

Coach Gurgin's expression was pained. "She's fought before and won, but the doctors think this time will be harder. Much harder."

"I'm sorry to hear that." My words weren't enough, but no words could be. Family and football—those were the two most important things to Coach. Now he was definitely losing one, and he might lose the other as well. My hands involuntarily clenched into angry fists. It wasn't right.

"Thank you," Coach Gurgin said. "I'd hoped to address the team before the news was released, but the damn media caught wind of it. I'm not yet at liberty to say anything officially."

In other words, he was breaking the rules by talking to me. He was already quitting, though, so it wasn't like the university could fire him.

"I understand," I said. "I appreciate your consideration."

"The program will be fine," he said. "Sometimes change is good." Though he said the words, his tone was sad. He wasn't ready to leave either.

"With all due respect, sir, you took us to a national championship. The program doesn't need change." *It needs you.* But damn it, I couldn't say that to him. As pissed as I was about the situation, it was much worse for him than for me.

He chuckled. "You took yourselves there. I was along for the ride."

The conversation transitioned into uncomfortable small talk for the rest of my visit. Long after I left, his words echoed in my mind—*change is good.*

Sometimes. Maybe. But change wasn't how I wanted to end my college football career. I was glad to know Coach Gurgin hadn't intentionally screwed me over, but it didn't change the facts.

I was really beginning to think I'd messed up by not entering the draft now while I was on top. I was the quarterback of the national championship team. The odds of us going all the way again next year were shrinking by the second.

Damn it. Four and out had been my plan. I'd wanted to take full advantage of the college system before going pro, but I'd also wanted to get my degree. When Freddie declared, I'd flirted with the idea of going with him but decided to stay the course. I hadn't wanted to make a rash decision. But now I was questioning my plan and wondering if I'd been shortsighted.

The thing was that it didn't matter at that point. My path was set whether I liked it or not.

* * *

Katie

WHEN WYATT CALLED and asked if I wanted to hang out, my answer was unequivocally yes. Not only did I want to see him again, but I'd taken my first MCAT practice test. My results were enough to send a Pollyanna running for the hills.

Okay, that wasn't quite right. My score was at the low end of the average range, but that wasn't good enough. My med school applications needed to be pristine, which meant an average MCAT score wasn't going to cut it.

I quickly parked, but as I approached Wyatt's apartment, nerves set in. We'd texted back and forth all week—some of the conversations scandalous—but subtext was difficult to discern from texts. When he pulled me through the doorway and kissed me hungrily, though, no subtext was needed. After we came up for air, I grinned at him. "If I didn't know better, I'd say you missed me."

The edge of his mouth quirked up into a half-grin. "So what if I did?" His eyes lowered, and when he lifted his gaze to mine again, it was smoldering. "Did you miss me back?"

At first, I tried to come up with a witty retort, but I decided on the simple truth. "I did."

With one last kiss, he released me, and the disappointment was bitter. I loved being in his arms, and if things had immediately led into the bedroom, I would have been more than okay with that.

Instead, Wyatt sprawled on his couch, and I noticed he seemed uneasy. His jaw was tense, and his fingers tapped the back of the couch. For a second, I wondered why he'd invited me over if he was in a bad mood, but then I shook off that thought. This wasn't about me—it was about the boy I'd begun to care about.

"Is everything okay?" I asked.

"I went to see Coach Gurgin today," he said. "It's not yet official, but he's retiring."

I sat next to Wyatt and put a hand on his knee. "I'm sorry. I take it the news was unexpected."

"I've heard rumors about it, but he confirmed it. He wasn't expected to retire anytime soon. I understand his reasons, but I wish he'd made the call a month ago."

I could tell Wyatt was second-guessing himself. I knew firsthand how much that sucked. The first year after I left acting, I'd had doubts that I'd made the right decision. Kassidy had moved on to other projects and was making a name for herself as an individual rather than a Sterling sister. It had been too easy to fall into the trap of wondering if I'd made the wrong choice, especially when I was having a rough time fitting in at school.

"Would it have changed your decision about the draft?" I asked.

He rubbed his fingers over his eyes then in circular motions over his temples. "Maybe. I don't know."

"You made the best decision you could at the time," I assured him. The truth was I didn't know that for a fact, but I knew enough about Wyatt to know he wouldn't make a decision without considering all the variables.

"Yeah, but what if it turns out to be the wrong one?"

"You can't think that way. There is no *right* decision—there's only a best decision at the time." It was the mantra I'd adopted six years ago, and I still used it today.

Wyatt studied me. "Why do I get the feeling you know what you're talking about?"

I averted my eyes. He barely knew me, yet he still saw me so clearly that I wondered if he could see my deepest secret, the one I hadn't even told my girlfriends. He made me feel exposed, vulnerable.

Luckily, his question was rhetorical. He continued. "I don't really want to talk about it anymore. It's all I can think about, and I want it out of my head for a while. So let's talk about anything but that. What did you do today?"

"I took a practice MCAT test."

He grimaced. "So what you're saying is your morning wasn't much better than mine."

I shrugged. "I don't mind taking tests. But I do mind not acing them." I was a sore loser, even when it came to tests.

"But you don't need that until next year, right?"

"I start applying to med school in the fall." That would have been the perfect time to talk about keeping things between us light and not getting serious since he had football and I had med school. But we were both already bummed out, and I didn't want to darken the mood.

Why would talking about things between us make our moods worse? It was the sensible course of action, yet I hesitated to broach the topic. Maybe I was overthinking things. That had to be it. There was no need to have a conversation about keeping things light because that would mean I thought we were getting too serious, which was ridiculous. Having "the talk" would make things unnecessarily serious.

Ugh. I was definitely making this way too complicated, at least in my head. Thank God I hadn't said anything to Wyatt. If he really could see into my brain, he would see how mental I was.

We've been on two dates. Chill the eff out.

"Where do you want to go?" he asked.

"UNC Chapel Hill," I said without hesitation. "They're one of the top-ranked schools, and it's close. A lot of the other really good schools are on the West Coast, and I don't want to go out there." *Shit.* I'd almost said I didn't want to go *back* there.

"Why? You don't like the cold, so it seems like California would be a good fit."

I shrugged. "I would prefer to stay in the east, so I'm also looking at UPenn or Pittsburgh. But honestly, I'm going to apply everywhere. It's so competitive. The acceptance rate for Chapel Hill is somewhere around four percent. And less than half of everyone who applies to med school every year actually gets in somewhere."

"You'll get in." He said it with such confidence that I felt reassured for a brief moment.

Then reality set in. "How would you know?" I laughed. "You haven't seen my transcripts or my test scores, which, if the practice test is any indication, won't be anything to write home about."

"I know you. And I know you're driven. So even if you don't get in the first year, you won't give up."

I didn't know how to take his comment. At first, it seemed like a backhanded compliment—that maybe I wouldn't be good enough the first time around but I was bound to get in eventually. It took me a second to realize that not giving up after failure was a win in his eyes. He'd paid me a compliment, no backhand involved.

I wished it were that simple in my eyes, but if I didn't get accepted my first year, I would feel like a failure. But would I push on? Definitely.

"Why med school anyway?" Wyatt asked.

"I want to do something important," I said simply. "I want to help people."

Wyatt fidgeted with the string on his sweatpants, which made it difficult to focus because a delicious sliver of his abs was on display. I wanted to trace the muscles of his six pack, to study them in the daylight so I could see if they were as glorious as I remembered. Hell, who was I kidding? Wyatt's body was ridiculously toned and sexy. I didn't need to see it again to determine that. I just wanted to see it.

"You don't want the money?"

It took me a second to register that he'd asked a question. I shrugged. "Sure, the money will be nice, but that's not the main reason."

Wyatt was astute to call me on my *I want to help people* line. While it was true, it wasn't the only reason I was pursuing medicine. Besides the fact that I'd always been fascinated by science and anatomy, it was the most respected profession I could think of. It wasn't that I considered acting not respectable, but, well... Kassidy had orchestrated a vag pic because she thought it would help her get ahead. I wasn't naive enough to think politics weren't involved in climbing the ranks in the medical field, but at least at the end of the day, I would be proud of my work, and people would respect me for the right reasons.

"Money helps," Wyatt said. "Try to tell me you'd go through all that school and the craziness if the job didn't pay well."

I hesitated, trying to formulate a response without flat-out lying. The truth was that thanks to *Sisters Squared* and my dad's smart investing, I would never have to worry about money. I could take a minimum-wage job and still drive a Mercedes. Not that I drove a Mercedes. I was very careful not to flash my money around. That invited questions. Or maybe it wouldn't. People might just assume that my parents were wealthy, but the truth was that they'd been poor before Kassidy and I changed that for them.

"I'm fortunate to be in a situation where income isn't an issue," I said carefully. I hated that Wyatt probably assumed my parents provided my financial safety net. But I couldn't very well explain how I'd started earning my own money as a toddler.

Wyatt held my gaze for a moment. "You're lucky." There was no judgment in his tone, but I felt judged all the same. I wanted to tell him it wasn't luck—it was damn hard work and missing out on a normal childhood. It was my mother placing her interests in front of my own and pushing, pushing, pushing me until I broke. If that was luck, then I would rather smash a thousand mirrors.

From his comment, I could discern that Wyatt's childhood hadn't been as privileged as mine. It made me realize that I knew very little about his background. If I'd wanted to, a quick internet search probably could have enlightened me. But I didn't want to read a reporter's version of Wyatt's life. I wanted to hear it from him.

"You grew up in Fairfax, right?" I asked. That much I did remember hearing.

"Centreville, to be specific. After my dad left the league, we moved in with my grandparents. He... it took him a while to get over it."

I wasn't sure exactly what he was referring to, so I cocked my head.

He gave me a small smile. "Sorry. Sometimes I take it for granted that people already know certain things about me. My dad played for Cleveland for one season, but he had to retire after a severe back injury. He still walks with a cane."

"Wow," I said softly. I had so many questions. Mainly, they were related to how Wyatt could step onto the field again and again, knowing what it had cost his dad. "I'm surprised your parents let you play."

"It's just my dad and my grandparents," Wyatt corrected. Though his tone wasn't harsh exactly, it was clear that further questions weren't welcome. "But they couldn't have stopped me even if they'd wanted to." It didn't surprise me that Wyatt had been a strong-willed little boy. Although given his large frame, he probably hadn't been "little" for very long.

"When did you start playing?"

"I always played sports from the time I was a toddler. I was ten when I zeroed in on football. It would seem an obvious choice given my dad, but I actually started with baseball. I wanted to be different than my dad."

"And now?"

"I still want to be different." Wyatt's expression was determined. "I want to make it more than one season."

CHAPTER 15

Katie

LATER THAT NIGHT, Wyatt's plan was to kill me. That was surely the only reason he'd insisted on taking me to the gym to train. *With weights.* Not with the machines that made it brainless, but with hard-core metal weights, the kind that could kill me if I dropped them on my head.

"Some of the machines are good," he explained. "But sometimes they make you lazy."

I eyed the impressive number of plates, which indicated several hundred pounds, on one of the machines. I pointed. "That's lazy? If there were five of me, maybe I'd be able to lift that."

He shook his head. "That's not what I mean. With free weights, you have to pay close attention to form. The machines make it easier to forget. What part of your body do you want to work on?"

I looked down at myself, suddenly feeling self-conscious. We'd stopped by my apartment on the way to the gym so I could change into workout clothes. I wore yoga gear because that was my workout of choice. I didn't have to think about what part I wanted to work on—I just followed the instructor. But yoga was all about proper form, so maybe I wouldn't be as bad at this weight thing as I feared.

"Arms?" I figured that might be the most painless and the least embarrassing.

I thought wrong.

Wyatt hooked me up with a dumbbell that was much too heavy and instructed me to hold it over my head with my elbows close to my ears. He guided my arms up over my head. "Extend like this. Make your actions smooth. Don't jerk the weight around."

I nodded and tried to follow his directions to the letter. He stood behind me, watching me in the mirror and dissecting my movements. He was... *intense.* And distracting. God, he was sexy, and it appeared effortless. He had stubble on his cheeks, ratty gym clothes on his body, and a cowlick in his hair that wouldn't quit. But he also had a smolder that would incinerate a forest, and biceps that I knew for a fact could easily carry my weight.

Wyatt adjusted the position of my arms, and I redoubled my efforts to maintain proper form, which meant I did my best to ignore him.

But that was easier said than done, especially when the aforementioned smolder was focused one hundred percent on me. Heat shot to my core, and I tried to convince myself it was from the workout. *Yeah, right.* Sex with Wyatt Archer was like a freaking potato chip—one taste wasn't enough.

The first half of the set was easy, but my triceps were quivering by the end. I returned the dumbbell to the rack and pushed my hair out of my face. "Done. Now what?"

Wyatt grinned. "That was the first set. You have two more."

I kept my jaw from dropping, but just barely. He really was trying to kill me. I smiled back at him with clenched teeth. "Sure thing, coach."

With a chuckle, he leaned close to my ear. "You can call me that later." He trailed a lazy kiss on my throat as he moved away, like we weren't in the middle of the university gym, like there weren't witnesses. Granted, there weren't many since it was Saturday night. Most people in their right minds were elsewhere, but still. My knees were weak as I reached for the dumbbell.

Wyatt was definitely trying to kill me.

* * *

WYATT HAD BARELY closed his front door before he was pressing me up against it, his hot, wet mouth on my neck. I reached under his shirt to touch the abs I'd just seen him toning. We'd spent an hour at the gym, and while I was worn out, Wyatt had barely broken a sweat. He'd done four times what I had, yet he'd called it a "light workout." *Snort.*

Gasping as his hand found my breast, I warred within myself. "I'm all sweaty."

"I don't care. I'll lick all the sweat off your body."

Holy mother of all things. Yes, please. I'll take two. Wyatt was making it difficult to keep my dignity intact.

"Or we could do something different," he said.

I pulled back and looked at him skeptically. I wasn't spontaneous by nature, and the last time he'd suggested we do something, he had ended up punishing me in the gym for an hour. *Let's circle back around to the idea of you licking my body.*

Seeing my expression, he chuckled, and the deep, throaty sound hit me right in my core. "Shower. What did you think I was referring to?"

"I can never tell with you."

"I'll give you a big hint," he said with a sly grin. "Most of the time, I'm scheming for ways to get you naked."

No scheming required. But I kept that thought to myself, not wanting to give him the wrong idea. Still, I couldn't seem to help myself with him. All he had to do was look at me with his steely gaze, and my clothes seemed to fly off my body.

Though come to think of it, that wasn't such a bad problem to have.

In the bathroom, Wyatt turned the shower on then quickly stripped me of my tank top and sports bra. Kneeling in front of me, he put his mouth on my stomach, drawing lazy circles with his tongue.

I ran my hands through his hair, holding on as the pressure began to build within me. I yanked his T-shirt over his head and ran my hands along his broad, muscled shoulders.

He gently tugged at the waistband of my yoga pants, and I shimmied out of them. He groaned as they got past my hips. Again, I was wearing no underwear under my workout clothes.

"You're killing me," he said. His erection was evident under his sweats.

"I swear I own underwear. And I usually wear it."

Standing, he tore his gaze from my body to meet my eyes. "Rest assured I'm not complaining. Dying this way would be a good way to go."

His expression of wanting and adoration made me bold. I trailed my fingers along the slender line of hair below his navel and followed it below his waistband. He sucked in a breath as I wrapped my hand around the length of him and started to stroke.

"I can think of a better way to go," I said.

Abruptly, he lifted me and placed me in the tub. Seconds later, he joined me under the scalding spray. After taking a second to adjust the water temperature, he laced his fingers through mine and lifted my arms above my head. Pressing my back to the smooth tile, he ground against me. He raked his fingers down the length of my body, touching every inch of me. What he was doing to me combined with the steam was making it hard to breathe. I clung to him.

"You okay?" He wrapped an arm around my waist, holding me steady, and I had the intense feeling of being right where I belonged.

"Never better."

* * *

Wyatt

A NAKED, DRY Katie was phenomenal. But a naked, wet Katie writhing against me was enough to make me lose my fucking mind.

Water rolled down her breasts, gathering on her nipples before dripping off. I sucked one rosy bud into my mouth, taking pleasure in the fact that it grew even tighter as my tongue rolled over it.

Her moan made my cock pulse.

God, she was gorgeous. Abandoning her nipple, I stood straight and smoothed her wet locks away from her face so I could look at her. Soulful eyes and sensually full lips were a wicked combination. She was like heaven and hell all mixed into one.

And she was mine.

I kissed each eyelid then her nose before moving to her mouth. Slowing things down, I took my time kissing her, exploring her mouth and the exact shape of her tongue. My fingers traced the curve of her collarbone, the dip of her lower back, and the luscious arch of her ass. I wanted to memorize every inch of her.

But more than that, I just wanted to be with her. Being naked with her was perfection, but every other minute spent with her was pretty damn good too. She seemed to understand me, and I wanted to know all of her—her hopes, her fears, her dreams.

At the moment, I would start with her body. I would learn what her every breath meant, how to make her quiver with need, and how to make her explode. And it would be my pleasure.

I dipped my hand between us, relishing in how she gripped my shoulders when my fingers found her clit. I caressed the swollen nub and found joy when her hips started to move.

My fingers still working, I dropped to my knees and traded my hand for my mouth. I sucked on her, so damn content to be doing so that I barely registered her nails digging into my shoulders. Her thighs shook, and I reached up to grip her hips to hold her steady.

Her softness tasted like gold, and I couldn't get enough. I only wished she were splayed out on my bed so she could spread her legs wider for me and I could taste even more of her.

But there would be time for that later.

Holy fuck, I never tired of this girl. Giving her pleasure was my everything, and I barely cared about my own as long as she was sated.

"Wyatt." Her breathy moan of my name was better than a stadium full of people cheering for me.

My cock throbbed, and despite my earlier thought, I wanted to push into her, not because I wanted to get mine, but because I wanted to be inside of her—I wanted to be as close to her as possible. I wanted to feel her muscles clamp around me as she came.

Her breathing became more erratic, and she let out a little cry that was sexy as hell. When she broke and her body quivered, I only had one thought: *again*.

CHAPTER 16

Katie

WYATT AND I fell into a rhythm—texting during the week and hanging out on weekends, sometimes with Freddie and Angie, sometimes alone. But the nights always ended with just us.

In early March, Wyatt and I flanked Angie on his couch while we watched the combine. Though I was a football fan, I classified myself as only a casual fan. I didn't know the ins and outs of the game and pro league like Wyatt and Angie did. So while their eyes were glued to the screen, even when it wasn't Freddie's turn, my attention wandered. And though I'd brought my MCAT study materials, they stayed tucked in my bag because I didn't want to seem unsupportive.

"Is anyone hungry?" I asked.

"Always." Wyatt didn't take his eyes off the screen. The amount of food he consumed still amazed me. Then again, he worked out incessantly and was more active than anyone I'd ever known.

"I'm too nervous to eat," Angie said.

I patted her on the shoulder as I went to the kitchen. *Poor thing.* Freddie had left days ago, and Angie had been a mess since then—not sleeping, not eating much, and not able to focus. Though whenever Freddie called, she put on the guise of being her regular sassy self, telling him his worries were ridiculous.

In the kitchen, I poked around in Wyatt's refrigerator and cabinets to see what I could come up with. The bag of tortilla chips made me want nachos, so I took inventory of what else we would need. Heck, it was almost dinnertime. I would just run to the store and get everything for a Mexican-themed night.

I went back into the living room and donned my coat. "I'm going to run to Kroger to get stuff for nachos and a taco bar. Any requests?"

Angie answered immediately. "Lime salsa and those lime tortilla chips. I could eat those."

"You got it." I slipped out the door, grateful to get away for a few minutes. The tension was rolling off Angie in tidal waves, and it was starting to get to me.

I was walking down the first aisle of the store when my phone rang. Thinking Wyatt must have thought of something he needed at the store, I pulled it out. It was Kassidy.

Damn. I chewed my lip as I watched the phone ring. Normally, I let her calls go to voice mail so I could screen whatever craziness she was bringing to the table and decide when to deal with it. But it had been weeks since I'd heard from her, and even though her calls usually stressed me out, I missed her.

I slipped in earbuds and took the call. Almost immediately, I regretted it. Kassidy was sobbing. It wasn't that I didn't take her problems seriously or that I thought she was a drama queen—well, okay, she kind of was. It was just that I couldn't relate to her problems, and a lot of the time, they were caused by poor decisions she'd made anyway. I realized that was judgmental, but it was also the truth.

"Kass?" When she didn't seem to hear me over her own sobbing, I spoke louder. "Kassidy? Can you hear me?"

"Katie?" She sniffed. "I was waiting for your voice mail to pick up."

I cringed. I didn't know why I was surprised that she'd caught on to my normal tactic. Though she made a lot of dumb decisions, she wasn't actually stupid. Maybe that was why some of her life choices bothered me so much.

"I'm here," I said. "What's going on?"

"I didn't get the role."

Feeling like a horrible sister, I paused. I had no idea what role she was talking about. I honestly didn't remember if she'd even told me. "You're going to have to remind me which role you're talking about."

"The one for that movie based on that book that was everywhere last summer. *The Prodigy Prophecy*?"

I still didn't remember her telling me anything about auditioning for a role in the upcoming movie, but I was familiar with the thriller. It had held a position at the top of the *New York Times* bestseller list for most of the previous year and was featured in several celebrity book clubs. Though I'd heard of it, I hadn't actually read it.

"Okay," I said. "Go on."

"I got called for a second audition last week, and I thought for sure I had a good shot. But I just heard that they're going in a different direction. They want someone more authentic." The sarcasm was laid thick on the words "different direction" and "authentic." It sounded like the director had given her a BS line to let her down easy, which sucked. It was patronizing. Kassidy was like me in that she preferred straight shooting.

"Authentic?" I frowned as I surveyed the tomatoes. "What does that even mean?"

"They want an actual college student. Instead of going with experienced, professional actors, the director wants to cast unknowns. It's bullshit. I really wanted that role. I would *kill* that role."

Casting unknowns had been a trend in Hollywood over the past year. Directors liked to take no-names and claim they'd "made them." It was a total ego stroke for them, but that was Hollywood. The director's words took on new meaning. Perhaps they weren't just bullshit.

"Aww... I'm sorry, Kass. But you know it's not about you, right? You can't control the whims of the director."

"If I were good enough, he might not have made that decision. If I had wowed him enough in the audition—"

"You can't think that way."

"Then how am I supposed to think?" she snapped.

I sighed. "You'll only drive yourself crazy wondering what could have been."

She sniffed. "I guess you would know."

I sucked in a breath, feeling like I'd been slapped across the miles. "What's that supposed to mean?"

"I don't mean anything by it. But you have to wonder what could have been if you hadn't quit."

I tossed a head of lettuce in my hand like it was a softball. "Of course I wonder," I acknowledged. "But it doesn't drive me crazy. I'm happy with my life." *Especially now.*

Kassidy mumbled something, and it sounded like "I'm not."

"What was that?" I asked. "I didn't hear you."

"Nothing."

Silence filled the line, and for the first time since I could remember, it was awkward. "What are you doing tonight? Are you going out with Tate?"

"We're not seeing each other anymore. His publicist thinks the pictures hurt his reputation and told him to distance himself from me."

Ouch. "That's too bad."

"I don't care. He doesn't matter."

I wondered who she was trying to convince. As good as my sister was at portraying a character's vulnerability on screen, she very rarely let her own peek through her tough exterior.

"Maybe we can get together this summer," I said. "It's been a while since we've seen each other." *Three years.* Her filming schedule had conflicted with my school breaks, and to protect my anonymity, we didn't visit each other's homes, which made seeing each other more complicated.

"It looks like I won't be working, so yeah, probably."

"Pick a place."

"Maybe we could go to Atlantis. We haven't been there since we were kids. Do you remember that? Mom was sure she'd seen Steven Spielberg, so she dragged us around the resort, looking for him." Kassidy laughed.

"Yeah," I said softly. I didn't remember it quite as fondly as she did. It was one of my first realizations of how desperately driven my mother was. She'd ruined our family vacation in the hopes of convincing Spielberg to remake *E.T.* starring twin girls or some nonsense. She could be delusional at times. I hated to think that I'd escaped my mother's clutches, but I kind of had. Once it became clear I wasn't going to make her any more money, she'd had nothing to do with me.

The trip down memory lane was unexpected and unwelcome. I quickly rerouted myself to the present. There was no sense dwelling on bad memories. *Learn and move on.*

"Pick a date and let me know," I told Kassidy and ended the call.

When I got back to Wyatt's apartment, nothing had changed. Angie sat cross-legged on the couch, and Wyatt sat beside her with his elbows resting on his knees. His eyes met mine, and an expression crossed his face that I never grew tired of—he was happy to see me. He was never coy about it.

He got up and took the grocery bags out of my hands. "Is there more?"

I shook my head. "That's it. I'm going to cook. Is that okay?"

Grinning, he put his hands up, palms out. "I will never say no to a woman wanting to cook for me."

"You might want to wait to pass judgment until you've eaten my food," I joked.

"It can't be worse than Freddie's cooking. I swear he gave me food poisoning once." He grimaced and unwittingly put a hand on his stomach.

"Sounds legit," Angie said without taking her eyes off the screen. "That man is a mess in the kitchen."

"I can almost guarantee my food won't be giving you food poisoning," I said as I went into the kitchen.

I had just finished browning the ground beef when Angie shrieked. "It's time!"

I rushed into the living room and sat beside her, taking her hand in mine. Wyatt held her other one, and we all waited with bated breath as Freddie's name and picture flashed across the bottom of the screen.

The commentator read off a list of Freddie's stats, mentioning that he was part of a power duo at VVU. I snuck a peek at Wyatt, and his jaw was tight. *Damn it.* He hadn't talked about it with me again, but I knew his decision about the draft still weighed on him. I wished I could help him find peace about it.

On the screen, Freddie got in position for the forty-yard dash.

"Oh, sweet baby Jesus," Angie said. "I can't watch."

"Yes, you can, and you will," I told her, giving her the tough love that I'd seen her give Freddie. "Don't you dare close your eyes."

It seemed to do the trick. Her eyes widened like she was afraid to even blink. Then Freddie shot off, and it was over in less than five seconds. *Jeez.* It was a good thing she didn't blink.

The time *4.2309* flashed on the screen.

"That's good, right?" Angie asked. "Damn it, I should have memorized those damn stats."

Wyatt grinned. "He's going to be pissed. He's one hundredth of a second away from tying the record."

"Damn," Angie said slowly. Then her grin matched Wyatt's. "My man is fast." Her grin fell off her face. "But you're right. He's going to bitch about that hundredth of a second. I can just hear him now."

"He's the fastest one so far this year," Wyatt reassured her. "That should shut him up."

"Hopefully." Angie nudged me with her shoulder. "Thanks, girl. I know you probably have better things to do, and I appreciate you being here."

"Of course," I said. "Freddie is my friend too."

"I'll hold your hand next year when it's Wyatt's turn."

I laughed and avoided Wyatt's gaze. I tried not to think about next year or, hell, even next month. Wyatt and I still hadn't defined our relationship, and I wasn't ready to have that conversation. At the moment, I could almost convince myself we were keeping things light, that our tenderness in the bedroom meant nothing. But I wouldn't be able to ignore the truth forever.

I was falling in love with Wyatt Archer.

CHAPTER 17

Katie

WYATT GRIPPED MY hand as we walked down the icy sidewalk. Good thing, too, or I would have eaten pavement. Although he was leading the way, he didn't have to. The thumping beat of the bass could be heard several streets away. I hadn't been to a block party like this since freshman year.

The party was at a row of townhouses. It looked like out of the dozen in the row, nine were participating. I felt bad for the people who lived in the three homes with the darkened porches. Hopefully, parties like this weren't a regular occurrence.

"Which one is your friend's?" I asked.

"I think it's the third one," Wyatt answered. "But he's not really my friend. He's a teammate. I don't know him well."

A pair of freshman girls streaked by with red cups in their hands, leaving a trail of giggles in their wake. I hoped they looked out for one another, but I didn't see how that would be possible if both of them were drinking. Just two years ago, that could have been me, Rachel, Destiny, and Danielle. Usually, I had ended up being the babysitter for the group.

"A lot of us said we'd come," Wyatt continued. "Like a bonding experience or some shit." Leaning down, he whispered in my ear. "I'd much rather be with you at my place than here."

Me too. Despite the cold, heat spread through my body. "Then let's not stay long."

He grinned down at me. "I just have to make an appearance, and then we can be on our way."

The townhouse he'd pointed out was packed full of people, and the smoke was visible from yards away. I inhaled. *Cigarettes and pot. Ugh.* To each his own, but if I went in there, my hair and clothes would reek. My coat was dry clean only, so it would be a pain in the ass to deal with. But I didn't want to come across like a diva, so I sighed and prepared to hold my breath.

"You don't want to go in there," Wyatt said. It was a statement, not a question.

I cringed. "Is it that obvious?"

"I don't want to go in either," he admitted. "A fair number of the guys smoke, but I don't get it." Wyatt treated his body like the well-oiled machine it was. He would never do anything that would compromise his performance, like contaminate his lungs.

I spotted a girl a few houses away who had lived in my hall freshman year. I pointed. "See the girl in the red hat? She's an old friend. I'm going to go catch up, and you can find your teammate."

"Are you sure?" he asked. "I don't like leaving you." He scanned our surroundings with precision, like he was rooting out any unfortunate guy who might try to hit on me. *News flash!* I'd had guys hitting on me long before he came into the picture. I was more than capable of handling unwanted attention. Still, though, I appreciated Wyatt's protective streak. Heaven help the fool who checked out my ass with him around.

"I'll be fine." I went up on my toes and pressed my mouth to his so he would know what was waiting for him. "But hurry back."

As I started to walk away, he yanked me toward him. His eyes raked over my face before he crushed his lips to mine, his tongue slipping in to massage mine. When he pulled away, I was breathless.

"Don't worry," he said. "I'll be back soon."

Before I could tell him I wasn't worried, he was gone. If he was concerned about leaving me by myself, he probably shouldn't have kissed me senseless before he left. I took a moment to collect myself then set off to find my friend Beth.

Her eyes widened, and she pulled me in for a big hug. "Oh my God! I haven't seen you since... since when? Has it been since the dorms?"

"I think so." At first, I felt like a jerk for not keeping up with her, but she hadn't kept up with me either, so whatever. I asked about her major since she'd been undecided, and she went into a long spiel of how she'd changed majors several times already, which meant she probably wouldn't graduate on time. The whole time she was talking, the girl she was standing with glared at me.

I gave the girl an apologetic smile. I hadn't meant to crash their party, but, well, it *was* a party. I hadn't done anything rude. When Beth finally stopped talking long enough to take a breath, I held my hand out to her friend. "I'm Katie."

"Sorry!" Beth said. "I'm the worst at introductions. This is Sonya. If you couldn't tell, Katie and I were in the same hall freshman year."

Sonya continued to glare at me. She reminded me of Regina George from *Mean Girls*—straight blond hair, smartly dressed, and a Queen Bee attitude. If I were Angie or Kassidy, I would probably ask her what her problem was, but I preferred to avoid conflict.

"I saw you with Wyatt," she said finally.

I nodded, not sure what to say because I *was* with Wyatt. He'd staked his claim on me loud and clear.

Sonya's lip curled. "You're not special, you know."

Beth gaped at her friend. "What the hell, Sonya?"

She shrugged. "It's the truth. I'm doing you a favor. Sisters before misters and all that."

This chick had totally gotten the spirit behind that saying wrong, but I wasn't going to point that out to her. I had no time for people like her.

"Well, thanks for the advice." I turned to leave, but Wyatt had come up behind me.

He planted a kiss on my lips and smiled at Beth and Sonya. "Hey, ladies."

Sonya narrowed her eyes at him and shook her head. "You don't remember me, do you?"

The blank look on Wyatt's face answered her question.

"Fuck you." She gave him one last dirty look before stomping off.

It didn't take a genius to figure out why she was pissed at Wyatt. I usually liked to have the full story before passing judgment, but since Wyatt didn't even remember her, it was doubtful I would get it. I didn't blame her for being pissed. I would have probably been angry, too, except I never would have slept with a known player in the first place.

Except I had. I shook off the uncomfortable thought. The situations were completely different.

Beth looked everywhere but at Wyatt. "Well, that was awkward. Catch you later, Katie." She disappeared into the crowd. *Nice to see you too, old friend.*

Closing my eyes, I took a deep breath. Given Wyatt's past, something like that was bound to happen eventually. Come to think of it, though, we didn't spend much time out in public. It didn't bother me—in fact, I preferred it—but now I had to wonder if there was a reason for it. How far and wide did his harem stretch?

"Katie..." His voice was thick.

I stared at him, wanting to ask so many questions, like if he really couldn't remember that girl and how many other girls there had been. But I couldn't delve into his past without disclosing mine, and I wasn't ready to do that. I hadn't carefully constructed my life around my secret only to give it away now. I trusted Wyatt—*loved* him even—but the risk was too great. And anyway, it didn't matter. His life was leading him toward fame, and that was a road I wouldn't take again. Eventually, we would have to go our separate ways.

The only question was once we were over, would he forget me too?

* * *

Wyatt

FUCK. JUST FUCK. My night had gone from bad to worse.

Some of the freshmen on the team had been partying way too hard. Drinking and smoking a little pot were one thing, but those fools were popping Ecstasy. Not only that, but they were doing it at a goddamn block party. It was a recipe for disaster. Best-case scenario was incriminating evidence showing up on social media. The worst case was the party getting busted by the cops and them getting their asses hauled in.

The last thing I needed was to get photographed with those idiots doing drugs. So I did my best to warn them, and then I got the hell out of there. I hadn't wanted to go to the damn party anyway, so it was no hardship to take Katie back to my place and spend the night with her. It was what I'd wanted to do in the first place.

But seeing that blond girl—I didn't even know her name—had ruined that. She'd looked vaguely familiar, but so did dozens of girls on campus. I easily could have sat next to her in class last semester. More than likely, she was a one-night stand.

Fuck me.

Except that girl had already done that. And now she'd fucked me over. *Christ.* I'd never regretted my past actions more than at that moment. I looked over at Katie in the passenger's seat. She was staring straight ahead. We hadn't spoken much since the incident, and though it had only been about ten minutes, it felt like forever.

"Do you want to talk about it?" I cringed as soon as the words were out. I hated how that made me sound, but her silence was killing me.

"No."

Well, shit. Even though Katie had never seemed interested in my past, that wasn't the answer I was expecting.

"Are you upset?" I asked.

"No." Her answer was followed by more silence.

Fuck. One-word answers definitely meant she was pissed, right? Where was Angie when I needed her? I didn't speak pissed-girl language.

"It seems like you are."

Sighing, she fiddled with her coat's zipper. "I'm not upset. Not exactly. I just need time to think."

I was done trying to translate her words. "What does that mean?"

She crossed her arms and looked out the window. "It means you should take me home."

This is not okay. I needed to fix this.

"That girl meant nothing to me."

Katie let out a sharp laugh. "Oh, that much was obvious."

Holy hell. I'd made it worse. "I slept around. I admit it. It's not something I'm proud of. But I don't do that anymore."

She gave me a sideways glance. "If I thought you did, I wouldn't be here."

Well, that was something. At least she didn't think I'd been cheating on her. I'd never cheated by default because I'd never committed to a girl until now. Though, technically, we didn't have a formal commitment.

"Katie—"

"I really don't want to talk about it right now. Please just take me home."

That was the last thing I wanted to do. I was afraid that once she got out of my car, I wouldn't see her again. It was a shitty feeling. Though I'd never wronged Katie, it seemed like karma had finally caught up with me.

* * *

Katie

WATCHING A VINTAGE Matthew McConaughey in *How to Lose a Guy in 10 Days* would normally have had all four of us girls sighing. But Rachel, Danielle, and Destiny weren't even watching it. Instead, they all looked at me like they wanted to say something.

I paused the movie. I sure as hell wasn't in the mood for a rom-com anyway.

"What?" My tone was sharper than I'd intended, but I refused to let myself feel bad about it. Three sets of eyes had been boring into me for the last half hour. I had a right to be a little testy.

"Rachel told us you and Wyatt had a fight," Destiny said.

I turned toward my BFF. "What the hell, Rachel?" And it wasn't even a fight. It was more like a non-fight—a rift. No angry words had been spoken.

Rachel hugged a throw pillow to her chest and shrugged. "I'm worried about you."

"I'm fine," I snapped.

Destiny snorted. "That right there is not the definition of fine. You've been happier than you've ever been, and now you're all bitchy."

"*Des!*" Danielle hissed.

Destiny's expression was unapologetic. "It's true."

I put a hand over my eyes and counted to ten. Then I tried to see the situation from their points of view. True, when Danielle had asked to borrow a white shirt because she hadn't had time to do laundry, I might have been a *bit* aggressive when I'd told her no. But what did she expect? Last time she borrowed my clothing, it came back with a huge wine stain on it. And *maybe* I'd forgotten to meet Destiny for lunch on campus on Tuesday like we usually did.

Aww, hell. I'd been an even shittier friend than normal. Poor Rachel. I couldn't think of any specific instances in the last few days when I'd been rude to my roomie, but no doubt I'd been a bitch to her.

"I'm sorry," I said. "I've had a lot on my mind."

"Ya think?" Destiny rolled her eyes. "What's going on?"

I didn't want to talk about this with them any more than I'd wanted to discuss it with Wyatt. But they'd been my friends for years, and I couldn't easily write them off like I'd done with him.

Sighing, I told them about the incident with Sonya at the party. The truth was that I had moved past that. Wyatt's promiscuous past was something he had to wrestle his conscience over. It didn't concern me.

But the incident had gotten me thinking about other things, like where we were going. More specifically, where we *couldn't* go. The thought of being just another girl in Wyatt's bedroom highlight reel felt like fingernails digging into my heart. But I couldn't be more than that. Wyatt was destined for fame, and that was a deal breaker for me. I could only imagine the media frenzy that would occur if the hottest new pro quarterback was linked to the long-lost Katelyn Sterling, beloved child star.

Just thinking about the flash of the paparazzi's cameras made my palms slick and my heart race.

"I'm not saying I approve of how much he slept around," Danielle said gently, "but, well, you knew about that when you started seeing him. I understand the scene with that girl was probably embarrassing, but does it really matter?"

This was why I didn't want to talk about it with them—because I couldn't explain what my real problem was. Katelyn Sterling was my guilty little secret, even from my friends.

"Here's what I don't understand," Destiny said. "You said he wanted to talk about it, right?"

I nodded.

"So why didn't you?"

"I needed time to think."

"And?" Destiny asked expectantly. "What are you thinking?"

I'm thinking I can't tell you what I'm thinking. But even if I could, would they understand? Would they understand why I'd kept this from them all this time? Or was I being totally and utterly irrational? The thing was that once the cat was out of the bag about my past, there was no putting it back in there. Maybe it would be no big deal, but I didn't know that for sure. Keeping the secret didn't hurt anyone, but telling it had the potential to ruin me. The thought of going back to that life—the paparazzi, the media scrutiny, the gawking—twisted my stomach and filled me with dread.

It was a risk I wasn't willing to take.

CHAPTER 18

Wyatt

I DIDN'T HEAR from Katie all week. We hadn't been one of those overly codependent couples, but I hadn't realized how much I'd come to anticipate her texts. *Shit.* Did that mean we'd broken up? We'd never defined our relationship, so I didn't know if she even considered me her boyfriend. Now I wished I had defined us. Though I didn't give a damn about the labels. I just wanted her.

Emptiness filled my chest, and I fucking hated it. Scowling, I pounded raw chicken breasts with a mallet. My life had done a complete one-eighty, and I'd turned into a sap, pining over a girl. I should go out with the guys that night and find another one to take my mind off Katie.

But that was the old me. The old me wouldn't have given a shit if a girl blew me off, which had never really happened anyway. It didn't matter because hooking up with a random girl wouldn't take my mind off Katie—it would only remind me of what I was missing. Besides that, there was no way in hell I would do anything to jeopardize whatever chance I had of Katie forgiving me. But since she wouldn't talk to me, I wasn't entirely certain what I needed forgiveness for.

I moved the chicken breasts into a pan and sprinkled seasoning on them. What a sad way to spend Friday night—meal prepping for the coming week. But what else was I going to do? I was kidding myself if I thought I was in the mood to go out.

Someone pounded on my front door. I shoved the chicken in the oven and went to answer it.

Looking disgruntled, Freddie stood in my doorway. "What the hell, man?"

I'd ignored his texts and calls all day. He wanted me to go out and wasn't accepting no for an answer. Normally, I would cave, but not this time. I didn't care if he was leaving town for good soon. *All the more reason for me to be in a shitty mood.*

"I'm not going out," I said. "I've got chicken in the oven." *Christ. So lame.* I was a regular Betty Crocker.

"I'll wait." Freddie came in and splayed on my couch, making himself at home. Annoyed, I shut the door behind him. His tenacity on the field was a thing of beauty, but in life, it could be a pain in the ass. He couldn't take a fucking hint. Hell, not even a hint—I'd flat-out told him what the deal was.

"I'm not in the mood to go out tonight."

His gaze assessed me, which only pissed me off more. It was like we were in some reverse shrink session, with him on the couch and me standing. "Just call her, man. Just call her and eat crow or do whatever you gotta do and put yourself out of your misery."

If I thought she would take my call—and if I knew what to say—I would. What kind of a jackass did he take me for? I turned my back on my friend and walked into the kitchen.

He followed me. *"Call her."*

"Stay out of it."

Ignoring me, he leaned against the refrigerator. "I've managed to keep my woman around for years. Don't you think you should listen to me?"

All his comment did was remind me of what I was missing out on. I checked the chicken, even though I knew damn well it wasn't close to done. "If I wanted your advice, I would ask for it."

"You might not want my advice, but you need it. Your head is all up in your ass right now."

I stepped to him. I'd never wanted to smash Freddie's nose in, but there was a first time for everything. "Back the fuck off."

Freddie looked down at his feet and shook his head. "Enjoy your chicken." He stalked off.

"I will," I muttered to the sound of the front door slamming.

I watched the oven timer count down. *Seventeen minutes to go.* Then I would package up the chicken into single-serve portions and stow the containers in the fridge. And then what? I'd already worked out once that day. My muscles needed recovery time. Watching TV was out—I didn't want to be tempted to tune in to the nonstop coverage for the upcoming draft.

What I wanted to do was what I'd done nearly every Friday for the last two months—spend it with Katie. She'd made it clear that wasn't going to happen.

Twelve minutes...

The more I thought about it, though, the more pissed I got. She owed me an explanation. I wasn't some one-night stand. I would be damned if I let her dismiss me like I was one.

Nine minutes...

Perhaps she was better off without me. I didn't know, but what I did know was that I wasn't better off without her. Pretty much the only times I felt centered, calm, and happy were when I was with her.

Five minutes...

I could treat her right. I hadn't been treating her poorly, but I could do better. We spent most of our time chilling in my living room and exploring each other in the bedroom. Maybe she wanted more. I hadn't thought I would be able to give her more than I was, but I realized that wasn't fair. Katie deserved everything, and I wanted to be the one who gave it to her.

One minute...

Hell. Freddie had gotten it almost right. I didn't need to call her—I needed to go see her.

Beep, beep, beep!

I yanked the pan of chicken out of the oven so fast, I nearly burned myself. Then without even grabbing a coat, I raced out the front door before I lost my nerve.

* * *

Katie

PRINCESS BUTTERCUP'S MOUTH was dangerously close to my spoon. I glared at her. "Oh no, missy. We are not having a *Lady and the Tramp* moment." I turned my body to guard my bowl of ice cream and spoon from her prying gaze. She licked her lips. *Do cats even have lips?* I didn't know, but I did know they had big, pathetic cat eyes.

I sighed. "Fine, but you're not licking my spoon." I got up from the sofa and walked to her bowl. Then I dumped a few spoonfuls of vanilla ice cream in for her. She pounced immediately. "For the record, I'm the Lady, and you're the Tramp."

Ignoring me, she flicked her fluffy tail.

"You're *definitely* the Tramp," I muttered as I plopped back down on the couch.

"Did you say something?" Rachel called from her room.

"Nope!" I yelled back.

Rachel appeared in the living room a minute later. She gestured to her outfit—a pink skirt, sheer black top, and leather ankle boots with dangerously high heels. "What do you think? The pink doesn't clash with my hair, does it?"

Rachel was always paranoid about wearing pink, even though she insisted her hair was auburn, which she also insisted was different than red.

"The skirt is too far away from your hair for it to matter," I assured her. "But even so, it wouldn't clash. I hear auburn-haired beauties can wear whatever color they want."

She grinned. "Whoever told you that is obviously a fashion genius."

"Where's Adam taking you?"

"No clue. He just said to look nice, so I'm doing what I was told."

I snorted.

She pointed a finger at me. "Shut it."

"I didn't say anything."

"Yes, you did."

"I made a sound," I clarified. "That's different."

Rachel rolled her eyes as we heard a knock at the door. Glancing at the wall clock, she frowned. "He's early. He's *never* early." She shook her hair out and opened the door.

Wyatt stood there, wearing jeans and a long-sleeved Henley T-shirt. His face was scruffy, and his hair was disheveled, though that seemed like it wouldn't be possible since it was so short. Yet he still looked ruggedly handsome.

I, on the other hand, was a hot mess. I was wearing my rattiest jeans, which had a stain on the thigh, and a long-sleeved T-shirt I'd stolen from my dad that read "May the Fourth Be with You." My hair was pulled back into a messy ponytail, which wasn't unusual, except I'd done it because I'd been too lazy to wash it... or maybe too depressed. Oh, and I couldn't forget to mention the film of cat hair that covered me from head to toe.

Rachel stepped back and looked at me with wide eyes. "Um, it's for you."

Ignoring the clenching and unclenching of my stomach, I stood. "What are you doing here?"

"I want to talk to you." His voice was rough and gravelly, like he'd had too many whiskeys. I peered at him, trying to determine if he was drunk or something. But he appeared completely sober. Showing up like this was out of character. Wyatt was nothing if not controlled.

I wrapped my arms around my midsection. "You could have called."

He narrowed his eyes at me with such focused intensity that I squirmed. "I *did* call."

Rachel's eyes were even wider now, and her gaze swung back and forth between us. "Um, do you want to come in?"

Wyatt stepped into our living room. "Thanks."

Princess Buttercup immediately started threading herself around his ankles and purring. *Traitor. If I could take back the ice cream treat, I would.*

"I'll leave so you two—" Rachel started.

"No, we'll go to my room," I said. "Adam will be here soon, right?"

Wyatt nodded to Rachel as he passed her on the way to my room. I shut the door behind us and faced him with crossed arms. But he wasn't looking at me. Instead, he was peering around the room, and I realized he'd never actually been in my bedroom. We always hung out at his place. I looked around the room self-consciously, my gaze landing on my unmade bed and my threadbare stuffed blue unicorn tangled in the sheets. Kassidy had its twin, but hers was pink.

I quickly straightened the covers on my bed and tucked the unicorn beneath the pillow. When I turned,

Wyatt was looking at me. My bedroom was decent-sized, but it felt crowded with him in it.

"I missed you," he said without preamble, his voice ragged. The statement was so raw and truthful, it took my breath away. What had it cost his pride to come and lay himself bare like this? I'd never meant to hurt him, but if I were honest, I hadn't considered that my absence would affect him so deeply. He was the Archer. He could have any girl he wanted.

Except me.

"I'm sorry," I said softly. "I needed time to think." I hadn't seen him in a week, and seeing him now made me more confused than ever. It was much easier to tell myself I could cut him out of my life when I wasn't with him. I didn't like the distance between us. It felt wrong.

"I don't know what to apologize for," he said. "I'm sorry my past slapped you in the face like that. But all of that was before I knew you."

"I know. I'm not mad about that. I mean… it's irritating, but it's not like you tried to hide it from me." *No, I'm the one with the secret.* But all it took was a trip to the grocery store to see all the magazines analyzing the amount of cellulite on the Kardashians' asses to remind me it was the right choice. *Outta sight, outta mind*—that was how I planned to stay until I could be sure no one would be interested in Katelyn Sterling. But I didn't know if I would ever be sure.

Wyatt looked totally lost and confused. "Then what are you mad about?"

"I'm not actually mad." If anything, I was sad, but I didn't feel like I had a right to bare that emotion to him, not when I was the one causing it.

He ran his hands over his hair, causing it to stick up even more and making me want to smooth it down. Hell, I just wanted to touch him, to soothe his heartbreak... and my own. But I was too scared.

"I don't get it," he said. "Things are—were—great between us. Or at least I thought so."

I sank onto the bed and put my hands over my face for a moment. "Coming face-to-face with your past made me think about the future. You know I don't like being in the spotlight. The attention you get sometimes when we're out gives me anxiety. I can't explain it." Well, I could, but I didn't want to. "It's not something I'm going to get over."

"I know," Wyatt said. "I figured that was why you were okay with staying in so much."

"But I can't stay in forever. *You* can't stay in forever. The life you're headed toward is not one that I can live with. So I wondered if it would be better—cleaner—to just end things now."

Before I fall even more in love with you.

The unspoken words hung between us. God, I wished things were different. But if they were, Wyatt wouldn't be who he was. I loved how passionate and driven he was. It was my misfortune that his path in life conflicted with mine.

Kassidy was the sister who made rash, passion-fueled decisions. Not me. The logical choice was to leave Wyatt while I still could.

He was quiet, his blue eyes clear and intense. Breaking up with him was so much harder than I'd thought it would be. It *hurt* so much more than I'd thought it would. The pain told me I was doing the right thing. Because the longer we stayed together, the more it would hurt.

Even now, the distance between us pained me. He looked so broken with his shoulders hunched, and I wanted to go to him, to kiss his hurt away. *To let him kiss my hurt away.* But that would be selfish.

"Why?" he asked.

My brow furrowed. "Why what?"

"Why would it be cleaner?"

I couldn't look at him. "Because I care for you. But I can't go where you're going. I just can't."

He was silent so long that I finally looked up at him. His jaw worked, and his eyes were stormy. *Shit. Is he pissed?*

"I don't believe you," he said finally.

I sighed. "I know a lot of people want fame, but trust me when I say that it's the last thing I want."

He shook his head. "Not that. The part about caring for me. Because this isn't how you treat people you care about."

His words stung. But a small part of me was pissed, so I homed in on that. "Really?" My voice dripped with disdain. "Maybe you should explain that to Sonya."

I could tell it took him a minute to catch the reference, and I realized he probably hadn't caught her name the other night.

His expression grew cold. "I didn't care about her. That's why I treated her that way."

My jaw fell open. I had no retort for that.

He stepped toward me. "That's my point. I was an asshole to girls in the past because I didn't care about them. For the most part, they didn't care about me. Not the real me anyway. But I care about you, and I want to know where I went wrong, where *we* went wrong."

The thickness of his voice and the pain in his eyes broke my heart. Because he hadn't done anything wrong except be himself. There was nothing he could do or say to fix things between us.

God, I wished there were. The thought of him walking out of my bedroom and out of my life made my chest tight. I tried to keep my composure, but my chin trembled, and my eyes filled with tears. If this was the right decision, then why did it hurt so much? *Logic is failing me.*

The anger on his face faded away. "Hey, it's okay," he said gently. "I didn't come here to make you cry."

His words only made the tears start to fall. My heart shattered. I didn't deserve him.

"Fuck, don't do that. I'll go. You never have to see me again."

"I don't want that," I said quickly before he could make good on his promise.

He stopped in his tracks. "Sweetheart, you need to tell me what you want."

"You," I blurted out. "I want you." I hadn't intended to say it, but it was like the fragments of my shattered heart took on a mind of their own, speaking out to salvage themselves. And I did want him. I wanted him so badly, it hurt.

He closed the distance between us with a fierceness he usually reserved for the football field and pulled me against him. "You have me." He crushed his mouth to mine, claiming me in a way that made it clear he wanted me too.

For a moment, I was in a dream, and all that existed was him and me and the perfect kiss. *Everything* was perfect. I had Wyatt, and all of my troubles faded away. But dreams couldn't last forever.

"Wait." I pulled away. "I can't make any promises beyond today. I can't—"

"Do you care about me?" he interrupted. "Do you want to be with me?"

"Yes," I whispered, "but—"

"It's a yes or no question." He smoothed my hair away from my face. "The rest is just details. We'll work it out."

* * *

Wyatt

I KISSED HER eyelids, then the tip of her nose, and finally her mouth, forcing myself to be slow and gentle when what I wanted to do was strip her clothes off and bury myself inside her again and again. *Mine.*

I wanted to give her candlelight and rose petals and soft music, but all I had was me. By God, I would show her how much she meant to me. *I would be enough.*

Wanting to free her gorgeous dark locks, I tugged on the band that held her hair back. When I made a mess of it, she laughed softly. "Let me."

While she untangled the wreck I'd made of her hair, I ran my tongue along the sensitive skin behind her ear. She tugged on my shirt, so I quickly pulled it over my head then stripped hers off followed by her bra.

With her breasts pressed against my chest, I felt that all was right in the world.

Even though her bed was only steps away, I slipped my arm under her knees and picked her up. Call me a Neanderthal, but I loved doing that. I loved how she fit so effortlessly in my arms.

I laid her down on the bed and ran my hands from her shoulder blades, over her breasts, and down to her navel, where I unbuttoned her jeans. She lifted her hips to shimmy out of them.

"Let me." I removed her hands from the denim and freed one lean leg at a time. Beneath the pants, she wore a simple pair of pink panties.

She propped herself up on her elbow and held her arm out toward me. My cock throbbed at the sight of her nearly naked and reaching for me. My heart swelled.

I wanted to kiss every inch of her skin. And when I was done, I wanted to do it all over again. I wanted to give her everything and more.

"I—"

Holy fuck. I was glad I didn't finish that sentence. I had been about to say *I love you*. I almost staggered backward from the weight of the feeling. I hadn't realized how deep I'd fallen, but I was gone for this girl. She was it for me. But I couldn't tell her. Not yet.

So instead, I worked my mouth over hers. I couldn't tell her, so I would show her.

* * *

Katie

I WAS CRAZY. I had to be to let Wyatt back into my life. Being with him jeopardized everything I'd put in place over the last six years to insure I could live a normal, fly-under-the-radar life. But my heart vetoed my head. It wasn't logical, but I didn't care. I wanted to be with him. I couldn't say how I would feel next month or next year, but for now, that was enough.

He pulled back, and his eyes locked onto mine. Everything inside me melted. But God, I was so scared. He wanted me to trust him, to trust that we would find our way. I didn't know if that was possible, but I wanted to try.

"Tell me what you want," he said.

"You."

"Be more specific."

I closed my eyes and forced myself to push my shyness away. "I want you inside me."

"Look at me when you say it."

I opened my eyes to find Wyatt staring at me intensely, waiting patiently. There was need in his eyes—not just physical but also emotional.

I licked my lips and swallowed. "I want to feel you inside me."

An expression I couldn't identify crossed his face, then he set to work fulfilling my desire by first removing the last of his clothing. He continued to kiss my body, but I cupped his face in my hands. Normally, I loved when he did that, but I was impatient to connect with him.

I gently pushed on his chest so he would lie on his back. Then I straddled him. He gripped my hips, looking up at me with a question in his eyes. I felt like so much in my life was out of control that I needed to be the one to take the lead in this moment.

I lowered myself onto him, one agonizing inch at a time. As I started to move, he put his fingers on my clit, and the sensation sent vibrations through my body. I clasped his free hand and held on as shock waves rushed through me. I threw my head back and gave in, digging my fingers into his chest.

While I was still feeling the aftershocks, Wyatt switched our position. Hiking my leg up, he plunged deep, and I gasped. His hand tenderly stroked my cheek, his gaze not leaving mine as he lazily moved inside me.

I buried my face in his neck, inhaling his scent. Three little words lodged in my throat, burning with their need to get out.

After he came, we held one another, not talking. Once he had fallen asleep, I studied his strong jaw and dark lashes that I loved.

There was so much more to Wyatt Archer than met the eye. He was kind, caring, smart, and ambitious. And he was mine. *For now.*

Careful not to wake him, I lightly kissed his lips. When I spoke, my voice was barely a whisper. "In case I never get another chance, I want to tell you just this once... I love you."

Chapter 19

Wyatt

A CAT'S ASSHOLE was inches from my face. *What... in... the... fuck?* The tail waved, its fur sliding across my face and making me want to sneeze. I squeezed my eyes shut and twisted my face away. What fresh level of hell is this?

"Princess Buttercup," Katie hissed. "Shoo! You'll wake up Wyatt."

This isn't hell. This is heaven. With a side order of annoying feline.

"Too late."

"Sorry. I don't even like this cat." Judging by the way she petted the animal as she said that, her words were a bold-faced lie. But I wasn't going to call her on it.

She stood and grabbed the cat, then trotted over to her door to let it out of the room. As she leaned down to put the cat on the ground, her perfect ass was on full display. *Morning wood? Check.*

Katie came back to bed, a slight blush on her cheeks, like she was suddenly shy. We'd been together plenty of times, but last night had been different. We'd crossed over from having sex to making love. Though neither of us had said the L word, I could feel it.

I was so in love with this girl. But hell if I was going to tell her that. She was spooked already, and I wasn't about to do anything to make her turn tail again and run. I had a feeling I still didn't have the entire story about why she wanted to call things off, but that didn't matter. What mattered was that we were together.

Now I just had to convince her to make the situation permanent.

But first, I was going to enjoy the moment. I'd never stayed the night in a girl's bedroom before. In the past, I'd always been sure to be out of there before the sun came up. Staying with Katie was nice, though. The bed was covered in soft things like throw pillows and extra blankets. But what was digging into my back wasn't a throw pillow.

I pulled out a blue unicorn with rainbow-colored hair and held it up. I grinned. "What's this?"

Katie snatched it and shoved it under the bed. "Nothing!" The word came out like a squeak, and her cheeks turned crimson. I'd forgotten how much I liked making her blush.

"It's okay if you still sleep with a childhood toy," I teased.

"I don't sleep with it," she protested. "It's just here."

Nope. Not buying that. But I didn't give her a hard time about it because I wanted to rib her for something else. She was so cute in the morning when her hair was tousled and she wasn't quite awake. The only thing that would make her cuter was a nice pink blush on her cheeks.

"You snore."

She gasped. "No, I don't."

I grinned. "You do. It's a soft, very ladylike snore. It's cute."

She looked horrified, and I laughed. What I'd told her was a partial truth—she'd snored for maybe a minute, but it had indeed been cute.

"The next time we sleep together, I'm going to stay awake and watch you sleep for a change," she said.

Ah, she caught me. I did like to watch her sleep. It was strange, and months ago if someone had asked me about the behavior, I would have said it was creepy. But I liked having my eyes on her no matter what. She looked so innocent when she slept, and all her walls were down. I needed to work on tearing them down while she was awake.

"You know I'm just teasing you, right?"

"So I don't snore?"

I laughed. "No, you do. C'mere." I pulled her on top of me.

She smiled down at me. "You're in a good mood this morning."

God, she was gorgeous, even with tangled hair and sleep crusties in her eyes.

"I am," I confirmed. "You make me happy."

Her entire body stiffened, making me glad I hadn't dropped the L word on her last night. She still had some issues to work through, and that was fine. But she wasn't getting rid of me, not when I was positive she cared about me.

"We should talk," she said.

"Talk." I gallantly didn't point out that I'd been wanting to talk all week and she'd been the one avoiding me.

"I don't want to lead you on—"

"Hey," I cut her off. "Do you want to be with me today? This week?"

"Yes."

"Then that's enough for now. I wasn't lying when I said that last night. As long as you're honest with me, we'll be okay." I expected her body to relax, but instead, she remained tense. Her expression became closed off. *Fuck.*

But she said, "Okay."

I forced myself to relax. The situation with my mother had fucked me all up in the head when it came to trusting women. But that was on me, not Katie. I couldn't let it cloud my judgment. Katie had said we were cool, so we were. *End of story.*

I picked up her hand and brought her fingertips to my lips, kissing them one at a time. The tension finally left her body, and she sighed and closed her eyes.

"I love when you do that," she said.

"What else do you love?" Now seemed like as good a time as any to remind her of everything good we had going for us, which was a hell of a lot.

She opened her mouth then closed it abruptly. "Are you fishing for compliments?"

I grinned. "Maybe." I pulled her toward me. "Come on. You can make me late for my workout for the first time ever. You're totally worth it, babe."

She let out an exaggerated gasp. "Now there's a compliment if I ever heard one."

She had no idea how right she was.

* * *

Katie

"I THINK IT'S a shotgun wedding," Wyatt told me as he merged onto the I-77 on-ramp.

I frowned. "Is that still a thing?"

He shrugged. "Maybe in the South. I don't know. All I know is the wedding was pulled together in about a month, so something is up."

Wyatt's buddy who'd graduated last year had been playing on North Carolina's practice squad, and we were headed to Charlotte for his wedding.

"Do you know the bride?" I pulled down the visor so I could use the mirror to apply lipstick, which I hadn't had time to do before running out of my apartment.

Wyatt shook his head. "Rob and I lost touch. I was surprised to get the invitation last week."

"Will you know anyone else there?"

He shrugged. "Maybe." He didn't seem concerned about it.

When Wyatt turned into the driveway, I gaped. *Holy shit.* This house was a legit mansion, with a huge round drive that circled a decadent fountain. Valets in tuxedos waited at the beginning of the line of cars.

As a woman climbed out of a car in a legit ballgown, I looked down at my simple black dress. "I think I'm underdressed."

Wyatt brought my hand to his lips. "You look amazing."

At least I'd curled my hair. I was out of practice, so it had taken much longer than expected. That meant we'd left thirty minutes later than planned. Luckily, Wyatt had given us a buffer, so we arrived right on time.

The valet opened my car door and held his hand out for me. Feeling somewhat ridiculous, I grabbed it and stepped out of Wyatt's beat-up Honda, which was out of place among all the luxury vehicles. When I was acting, I'd gone to a few red-carpet events, so the lavishness shouldn't have thrown me for a loop. However, going to a premiere for a Disney movie as a twelve-year-old was a lot different than attending an event as an adult.

When Wyatt walked around the car and offered his arm, he nearly took my breath away. Because I'd been running late, I hadn't gotten a good look at him when he picked me up. But now... *holy mother of all things.* The deep-charcoal suit was tailored to perfectly fit his tall, muscular frame. His tie matched the blue of his eyes, and somehow he'd managed to tame the cowlick in his hair. I didn't know how it was possible that a suit made his jaw look even more chiseled. Wyatt cleaned up well. More than well. He was delicious.

"Do you like what you see?" he whispered in my ear, laughter teasing his voice.

I blushed. With my acting background, I should have been able to better mask my ogling, but Wyatt's good looks sometimes took me by surprise. I knew he was good-looking and all that, but sometimes when I looked at him, it was like I was seeing him for the first time, like I was starting to fall in love with him all over again. It was a jolt to my system every single time.

We followed the walkway into the house, which put us in a large foyer. More staff in tuxedos waited to take our coats. I nearly tripped in my heels because I was craning my neck to take in the splendor of the house. It was obnoxiously opulent.

"Whose house is this?" I asked quietly.

"Rob's cousin," Wyatt answered. "He's a lineman for Carolina. He helped Rob get on the squad." He looked around, taking in our surroundings. "It's nice, right?"

"It's beyond nice." My dad and I had lived in a nice house—four bedrooms, three baths, and a pool out back. It was more than the two of us needed, and we had a cleaning service come once a week to keep up with it for us. But a house like this had to require full-time staff.

The wedding and reception were taking place in the backyard. When we stepped out the back door, though, it didn't feel like we'd gone outside. We were in a huge heated tent. Everything was white—the tablecloths, the chair coverings, the flowers, and of course, the tent. When the bride finally emerged, in her white dress, she would be camouflaged.

We stopped at a table with place cards and learned that we were at table forty-seven. And that wasn't even the last table number. When Wyatt had told me about the wedding, he'd indicated it would be a small affair. Or perhaps since he'd told me it was last-minute, I'd incorrectly assumed that.

A passing waiter held trays of champagne, and Wyatt took two for us. I gulped down half of it even though I didn't really like the bubbly stuff.

Wyatt eyed me. "Better?"

I nodded. "Much."

He flagged down a waiter who was handing out canapes and crackers with little mounds of caviar on them. He took several and quickly polished them off.

I raised my eyebrows. "I wouldn't have taken you for a caviar eater."

"Oh, is that what that was?" He shrugged. "I'll eat anything. I'm starving."

If it was a shotgun wedding and the bride was pregnant, like Wyatt suspected, I couldn't tell. She wore a tight-fitting mermaid-style gown with a sweetheart neckline. The ceremony was short and sweet. Wyatt held my hand throughout.

We were seated with some former VVU players, most of whom were there stag. I'd spent a fair amount of time with Wyatt and Freddie, but with all of these former linemen together, it struck me how big they were. Their hands were as large as the sizable dinner plates, which the waitstaff kept refilling. It seemed the wedding planner had been forewarned about how much football players could eat.

"Is it true Gurgin is retiring?" the only guy with a date asked Wyatt. Wyatt was the only current VVU player in attendance.

Wyatt nodded.

"Shit, man, that sucks. Any idea who's replacing him? Maybe they'll promote Franklin." Coach Franklin was the defensive coordinator.

"I don't think so," Wyatt said. "Gurgin's retirement leaked because of one of the candidates they're interviewing. If they were going to promote Franklin, they wouldn't bother with interviews."

The guy shrugged. "Maybe they have to go through the paces of interviewing people. Like red-tape bureaucracy shit. They could still promote Franklin."

"With Gurgin leaving, we'll be lucky if Franklin stays." Wyatt rolled his neck, cracking it. I wished the other guy would shut up. Wyatt obviously didn't want to talk about it, or at least that was obvious to me.

The DJ called the bride and groom to the floor for their first dance, and I was grateful for the distraction. I was even more grateful when he invited everyone to the floor and Wyatt held his hand out with a smile. We found a spot, and he wrapped his arms around me. As we swayed to the sweet melody of a country song I'd never heard before, Wyatt moved much more gracefully than I'd expected. Though I shouldn't have been surprised. He was good at everything.

Closing my eyes, I laid my head on his chest and allowed myself to get lost in the moment—Wyatt's scent, the feel of his body as it swayed with mine, the sound of his heartbeat. As the singer crooned about love lost and found again, I couldn't help but compare the lyrics to Wyatt and me. We'd had a little hiccup—a speed bump in our relationship. There was no reason we couldn't have smooth sailing for the next year. *But then what?*

My pulse spiked as anxiety filled me. Forcing myself to exhale, I recited my mantra in my head. *Live in the present. Enjoy the now.*

* * *

Wyatt

ON THE DRIVE home, Katie looked happy, which made me happy.

"Did you have a good time?" I asked. It was important to me that she did. I wanted her to feel like she fit into my life.

"It was one of the nicest weddings I've been to." She laughed. "Even if I didn't know the bride and groom."

"I don't know her at all, and I don't know him very well," I said. "But I thought it would be nice to go." Also, I wanted to show Katie what life could be like with me. "That house was amazing, wasn't it?" I glanced over at her so I could gauge her reaction.

"It was. It's more house than I'd know what to do with."

That was not exactly the response I'd been hoping for. It was odd. For so long, I'd written off girls who seemed overly interested in the finer things in life, figuring they just wanted me for a meal ticket. Now there I was trying to do the exact opposite—entice Katie with the promise of things to come.

I shrugged. "I don't think extra space is a bad thing."

"No, I suppose not. I wonder what the master closet looks like," she mused. "I bet it's magnificent. Closet space is something you can never have enough of."

"Yeah." But I didn't really care. I'd never been into clothes or fashion. As long as my ass was covered, I was good.

"By the way, Naomi is pregnant, so you were right about the shotgun-wedding thing. During the toast, I noticed they had some sparkling grape juice hidden under the table for her."

I nodded. "I figured."

"So I guess Rob will have to quit the practice squad now. That's a shame."

"Why would he do that?"

"He'll need a real job now that he's got a baby on the way."

I frowned. "The practice squad is a real job."

"Sorry. I meant a *paying* job. Babies are expensive."

I gave her a sidelong glance. "Practice squads get paid."

She blinked. "Really? I didn't know that."

"If he stays on all year, he'll clear six figures easy."

"Are you kidding me? That's twice the average US income. That's more than the average teacher makes." When I looked over at her, she shrugged. "I took econ last semester. Anyway, that seems excessive for the practice squad."

Her comments touched a nerve, and I found myself getting defensive. "It's no different than how Hollywood actors are paid."

"Actually, it *is* a little different," she corrected. "The practice squad is probably the equivalent of an extra, right? Extras are paid slightly more than minimum wage."

She was full of random information today. Too bad none of it worked to prove my point.

"But the big celebrities make millions."

"Yeah." She chewed on her lip. "Money can't buy happiness, though."

I thought of my mother, who'd left us to chase money. The last I heard, she had been dating a NASCAR driver. Of course, that was at least ten years ago. She'd been dirt poor growing up, and as a teen, she'd gotten by on food stamps and her pretty face. I could understand how an experience like that could turn someone into a gold digger. Of course, the same experience gave others the drive to make something of themselves. Not my mother—she had no ambition for herself. She'd just wanted a man who would take care of her.

I wondered if she'd ever found what she was looking for and if it had made her happy. Or had she come to the same conclusion as Katie, that money couldn't buy happiness? I didn't know if the saying was true or not, but maybe if my mother hadn't been in search of financial security, I would have known what it was like to have a mom who gave a shit.

"No, it can't," I agreed. "But it sure as hell can help."

CHAPTER 20

Katie

WITH THE UNIVERSITY spring game right around the corner, Wyatt was busier than ever, which meant I saw less of him. The game was a school tradition, an intra-squad scrimmage that pitted the up-and-coming players against the veterans. Though the game was technically for fun, Wyatt took it as seriously as he would a regular-season game. While I appreciated his dedication, I was miffed that he wouldn't let me spend the night before the game. It was only one night, though, and I'd better get used to it if we were going to be together in the fall. But summer was looming around the corner, and so far, I hadn't had any luck finding an internship in Bleaksburg. There weren't even any volunteer positions available at the local hospital. That meant I would be forced to spend the summer at home in Florida, where I knew the hospital would welcome my volunteer hours. With all the retirees in Florida, there was no shortage of health care facilities that could use help.

The morning of the game, Rachel and I went to Destiny and Danielle's apartment to prepare. Danielle had gotten face stickers with the VVU logo and orange ribbons to adorn our ponytails. The spirited atmosphere reminded me of the excitement I'd felt when we attended our first few college football games. Only this time, the excitement was because the Archer was my boyfriend.

It was so crazy. If someone had told me freshman year that I would wind up dating the quarterback who was already making a name for himself, I would have scoffed. Now I was giddy in anticipation of seeing him in action.

"Damn," Destiny said when we got to our seats. Wyatt had managed to get us seats in the lower half of the stadium, right on the fifty-yard line. "You should have dated him freshman year when we were up in the nosebleeds."

"He probably wouldn't have been able to get us tickets freshman year," I said absentmindedly. "He has a little more pull now."

Rachel rubbed her arms as she shivered. "Spring, my ass."

"It'll warm up when the sun hits us," I said. Our seats were currently in the shade.

Around us, the stadium slowly filled with fans, and the band filed in. We were very early, but I'd been paranoid about finding parking and getting to our seats on time. But now that we were just sitting there with the minutes counting down on the scoreboard, I was antsy.

Relax. This game doesn't mean anything. It's just a glorified scrimmage. Still, it would be an indicator of how the team would look in the fall. Though Wyatt had said he wasn't worried, I could tell he was.

When Wyatt charged onto the field, leading the team, my heart leapt. I screamed as if he could hear me above the roar of the crowd. *Holy crap, this is exciting.* Too giddy to stand still, I bounced on my toes. The girls grinned at me.

"That's my man," I said proudly.

The first play was a simple handoff, and Wyatt's team easily made the first down. On the sideline, Coach Franklin, who was acting as head coach for the new guys, railed at them for letting the runner through. On the other sideline, Coach Gurgin was the picture of calm. I looked at him sadly, knowing that would be the last time he would walk the field as head coach. Obviously, I didn't know him, but I felt for him.

The new guys settled down after the first few downs. Still, Wyatt's team slowly and methodically pushed the ball down the field. After he ran it in for a touchdown, he tossed the ball and headed toward the bench with no celebration. That was the intensity he was known for. That play was over, so he was already mentally preparing for the next one. He pulled off his helmet and stood next to Coach Gurgin. Meanwhile, the crowd chanted "Arch-er! Arch-er!" I'd heard it before, but this time was different. I could feel the roar in my chest, and it filled me with pride.

Rachel leaned in to whisper in my ear. "Is it weird looking at him on the field like that and knowing you'll probably have sex with him tonight?"

My eyes widened, and I looked around to make sure no one had heard. "Rachel!" I hissed. "What the hell?"

She shrugged. "That's what I would be thinking if I were you."

"That is *not* what I'm thinking about." Of course, now that she'd planted the seed, it was on my mind. God, those football pants were tight. I knew he wore pads on his legs, but there were no pads on his ass, and it was on full, *glorious* display. The next time he threw the ball, my gaze lingered on his biceps, which I was all too familiar with.

Rachel gave me a knowing look. "You're thinking about it now, aren't you?"

I shoved her playfully. "Shut up."

She laughed.

The new guys' possession was three and out, putting Wyatt back on the field. The first down was a throwaway—no receivers were open. His teammates got in a huddle around him, and he called the next play. The offensive line got into position, and Wyatt called for the snap. He stayed in the pocket and lobbed the ball down field when his man was in position. It looked like it was going to be at least a forty-yard gain.

Suddenly, a lineman on the new guys' squad slammed into Wyatt, hitting him so hard that his feet lifted off the ground. It was like I was watching in slow motion as Wyatt landed on the ground on his back. He didn't get up. My hands flew to my face, and I had to stop myself from screaming. Next to me, a man yelled, "Boo! Roughing the passer!"

Rachel put her arm around me. "He's okay," she reassured me. "He just got the wind knocked out of him."

But he isn't moving. He isn't moving. He isn't moving. He... Wait, there. He's breathing.

The center walked over to him and held his hand out. Wyatt used it to pull himself into a sitting position. He paused for a second then pulled himself upright. A ref trotted over to check on him.

My shoulders sagged as I sucked in air. Getting hit was part of football. But damn, it was one thing to know it, and another to watch the man I loved get laid out. Suddenly I didn't know if coming to the game had been such a good idea.

Destiny narrowed her eyes at me. "Tighten up," she said. "Your man can take a hit."

The ref turned his mic on. "Roughing the passer. Number eighty-seven, defense. Fifteen-yard penalty. Automatic first down."

The crowd cheered as Wyatt's squad moved fifteen yards down the field to set up for the next play. I wished Wyatt would take his damn helmet off so I could see his face. I needed to reassure myself that he was okay.

My phone buzzed, and I was tempted to ignore it, but I thought the distraction might help. It was a text from Angie.

Hard to watch, wasn't it? LOL. Don't worry. It gets easier.

I smiled. If there was one person who understood the emotional roller coaster I was on, it was her. I should have made arrangements to sit with her.

Tightening my ponytail, I squared my shoulders and braced myself for the rest of the game. If Wyatt was tough enough to take a hit like that and keep going, then I would have to be tough enough to watch.

* * *

Wyatt

THE GAME HAD been rough. A lot of the newer players were skittish and made dumb mistakes. That worked in my squad's favor for this game, but in the fall, those guys would be on my side. We had a long road ahead of us to get the team in shape for the fall season. But damn, it had felt good to get on the field again. There was something magical about college football. I was going to miss the rush of running out of the tunnel and knowing the people cheering were the same ones I sat next to in class every day. Some players considered college ball a step on their path to the pros, but I genuinely loved it. Perhaps that was part of the reason I'd been reluctant to take that next step.

Standing next to Coach Gurgin on the sideline, hearing his voice in my helmet, and knowing it was the last time had been bittersweet. When I'd learned he was leaving, I'd forgotten about the spring game. I was glad I'd gotten one last chance to play for him and do him proud.

As I turned into my apartment complex, I eyed the visitor parking spaces and was pleased to see Katie's car there. I'd given her my key so she could wait for me after the game. A small part of me had worried she wouldn't show. She was still holding part of herself back, and I wondered if one day she would decide to hold everything back. I was trying to be patient and give her the space she needed to work everything out in her head, but it wore on me. I was all in, and I'd known she wasn't quite there yet, but I hadn't realized it would bother me as much as it did.

Katie flung open my front door before I could put the key in and hurled herself at me in an imitation of the linebackers I'd faced that afternoon. Only Katie's hit was one I would gladly take any day. She flung her arms around my neck.

Chuckling, I wrapped my arms around her. This was different... nice. Normally, I came home to an empty apartment after games, but I could definitely get used to this kind of greeting.

She cupped my face in her hands and planted a kiss on my lips. "You were awesome."

"Thanks." It hadn't been my best performance, but it certainly hadn't been my worst either. I was already mentally playing the game reel in my mind to determine what I needed to work on.

"I wanted to kill that guy who took you down in the first quarter."

It took me a second to figure out what she was talking about. "Oh, Brewer? He doesn't hit that hard."

"It looked hard. You didn't get up right away."

"Just got the wind knocked out of me," I assured her. "I've had worse."

Anger flashed in her eyes. "It was a cheap shot."

We walked into the apartment, and I dropped my bag just inside the door. "He was skittish. They all were, especially in the beginning. Trust me, the last thing he wants to do is hurt me." I grinned, donning the confidence that was often mistaken for cockiness. "Without me, they're screwed."

She eyed me playfully. "I don't know. Keeley looked pretty good."

I snorted at the mention of the red-shirt freshman. He was probably the only one on the team who'd been hoping I would declare for the draft so he could take my place. He had potential, but he wasn't there yet. His ego impeded his ability to make smart plays. Hopefully the new coach—yet to be determined—would knock his ass down a few pegs.

"Are you hungry?" Katie asked.

"Starving."

"Great, because I made plans with Angie to have dinner with her and Freddie."

"When?" I asked.

"Maybe an hour?"

"Perfect."

She must have noticed the gleam in my eye because she shrieked and scooted away. *She's so cute, trying to evade me.* I caught her easily and threw her over my shoulder.

But to be fair, she didn't try too hard to escape.

* * *

AN HOUR AND a half later, we sat around a table at the local Mexican restaurant.

"I would have caught that pass." Freddie stretched his long legs out into the aisle. "It was a little wobbly, but I would have gotten it."

I rolled my eyes. "Wobbly, my ass."

"I don't know, man. Watching from the stands was a lot different than watching on the field. Maybe I'm seeing things differently."

Angie turned to her boyfriend. "Will you stop? You already told me how well Wyatt played. Why are you giving him a hard time?"

Freddie pursed his lips. "I'm just keeping his ego in check is all. Because I'm a good friend."

He was pissed he hadn't gotten to play in the game. He was itching to get on the field again. If the draft weren't next week, I would give him shit back, but that would open a can of worms I didn't want to get into. My boy was a mess.

Katie looked up from tapping on her phone. "I hope you don't mind. I told Rachel she could join us. She's right down the street."

When Rachel arrived, she flagged down the passing waiter and ordered a jumbo margarita. "Thanks for letting me crash your party," she said. "Adam stood me up again."

"Adam?" Freddie leaned forward. "Tell me his last name, and I'll go beat him up for you."

Rachel laughed. "Thanks for the offer, but I'll pass. One of these days, I'll wise up and kick him to the curb for good."

"I wish you would," Katie said. "He really is an ass."

Rachel shrugged and grabbed a chip from the basket.

"Do you know everyone?" I asked.

Putting a hand in front of her mouth, which was full of chips, she nodded toward Angie and Freddie. "We haven't officially met, but I know who y'all are. I'm Rachel, Katie's roomie and BFF."

Freddie drummed his fingers on the tabletop. "I don't have to actually beat him up. I could just scare him a little."

Rachel laughed, seeming to have already figured out that she couldn't take Freddie seriously ninety percent of the time. "Thanks again, but I'm good." She nodded toward me. "Great game today, by the way. Though I thought Katie was going to have a heart attack after that late hit in the first quarter."

"Now there's someone I should beat up," Freddie commented. "Those kind of mistakes lose games."

"Then it's better for him to work out the kinks now before the season starts. He'll settle in."

"Spoken like a true politician," Freddie said.

I shrugged. Maybe. But I wasn't one to talk shit about my own players out in public. Not only was I ethically opposed to it, but it was also a matter of self-preservation. Too many talented players had ruined their careers because of their off-the-field antics.

A few tables over, some girls kept looking at their phones then peering at us. *Damn it.* Two months ago, I wouldn't have even noticed, but now I was hyperaware of that sort of thing because I knew how much Katie hated it.

I shifted so that her view of the other table was blocked. If she hadn't already noticed, hopefully she wouldn't. But damn it, I couldn't shield her from prying eyes forever. Eventually she would have to decide I was worth dealing with the minor inconvenience. Either that or...

I wasn't going to think about the alternative. Right now, I was content. I'd played a good game that day, spent some quality time with Katie in the bedroom, and now I was unwinding while surrounded by my favorite people in the world. Plus Rachel. But I was sure she was good people, too. I just didn't know her well.

The girls who'd been checking us out came over to our table. *Shit. There goes my pleasant evening.*

"Is it true?" one asked. She held out her phone, but instead of putting it in front of my face, she showed it to Katie. *What the fuck?* That took things too far. It was one thing to talk to me, but they needed to leave her alone.

Katie went pale, and her glass slipped out of her fingers, landing on the table. Water streaked down the table, dripping off the edge and onto her legs. But she didn't even seem to notice as Rachel shoved a napkin in her lap to try to minimize the damage.

"I can't believe it," the girl said. "Katelyn Sterling goes to my school!"

Katie's mouth opened and closed as if she were trying to speak, but no words came out.

"What the hell?" I was pissed. What the fuck had that girl shown her? I grabbed the girl's hand and twisted it so I could see the phone's display.

It was a picture of Katie and me on the dance floor at Rob's wedding that someone had posted on social media. I hadn't been aware the photographer had had us in his sights, but whatever. That should have been no big deal.

But below the picture, someone had left a comment: *Look! It's that* Sisters Squared *girl with VVU quarterback Wyatt Archer.*

Sisters Squared sounded vaguely familiar, but I couldn't place the reference. I scrolled down and skimmed the comments. There was something about an MIT student using AI facial recognition and age-progression software to locate the child actor nobody had seen since the show wrapped. I scrolled farther and saw side-by-side pictures of Katie and the child star Katelyn Sterling. The resemblance was uncanny.

"Can I take a picture with you?" the girl asked Katie. "No one will believe me without it."

Katie stood up so fast, her chair fell over, but between the chair and the girls crowding around, there was nowhere for her to go.

"Daaaayyyy-ammmnnn, Katie," Freddie said. "You're a celebrity. You've been holding out on us. Hey, can you introduce me to Denzel?"

Her eyes were wide, and her chin quivered. In fact, her whole damn body seemed to be shaking. By that point, our whole side of the restaurant was staring, and many patrons had their camera phones pointed in our direction.

A flash went off, and it snapped Katie out of her stupor. She pushed past the girls and rushed toward the front door. I followed, catching up to her just outside, but I had to grab her wrists to get her to stop.

"Katie, wait." I was utterly confused. "What the hell is going on?"

"I knew this would happen," she whispered. Her eyes were wild, manic even. It was a side of her I'd never seen before. "I knew it." She yanked her wrists out of my grasp.

All of the pieces quickly fit together in my head. Katie hated the spotlight so much because she'd once been in it to the ninth degree. *Holy fuck.*

Tears were in her eyes. "Do you know how hard it was to start a new life? To keep my past hidden so I could be normal?" Her expression was angry, anguished, and irrational, which conflicted with the tears that had begun streaming down her face. *Damn it.* If she were just crying, I would know what to do. But I was at a loss.

I reached for her. "Katie—"

She moved out of reach. "No. This was a mistake."

CHAPTER 21

Katie

"I KNEW THIS was a mistake. I knew it, but I stayed with you anyway." I started pacing in a tight three-foot radius and wringing my hands so briskly, my skin was in danger of rubbing off. Though Wyatt stood in front of me, I couldn't see him. All I could see was the replay of that girl sticking her phone in my face and the flash of a camera.

Then the pictures in my head went further into the past. The hotel management office we'd waited in while the police took away the man who'd broken into our hotel room. A broken cake on the ground that had been a result of the scuffle between security and the paparazzi who'd crashed my thirteenth birthday party. The bathroom stall I'd hidden in to escape the jeers of my new classmates once I became Katie Sullivan, but they'd refused to see me as anything more than Katelyn Sterling.

All I'd wanted was to live a normal, nondescript life. Instead, I'd taken a risk on Wyatt, and it had blown up in my face. "This relationship is a mistake. I knew nothing good would come of it."

"Nothing good." Wyatt's voice was so quiet, I almost didn't hear him. Blinking, he took a step back. He ran a hand over his head, a bewildered expression on his face. Then his eyes hardened. "You lied to me."

What little composure I had left broke. "I lied to everyone!" I yelled. "I worked for years to put things in place so I could have a normal life, and just like that"—I snapped my fingers—"it's gone." I wanted to weep for what I'd lost, for the unfairness of it all.

"You lied to me," Wyatt said again softly. His tone indicated he was still wrapping his head around all the facts.

"I shouldn't have gotten back together with you," I said. "Being with you was a mistake. I knew it would end in disaster. I *knew* it."

Wyatt laughed bitterly. "I'm a mistake."

I wrapped my arms around myself. "You should have just let me go." I'd tried to do the logical thing, but instead, I'd given in to my emotions. I'd given in to Wyatt. I should have been stronger.

Wyatt stared at me, morphing into someone I almost didn't recognize. Anger and hurt blazed in his eyes. "That's what you want? You got it." He turned on his heel and went back into the restaurant.

Allowing misery to wash over me, I hung my head. *Shit. Now what?*

The distinct click of someone snapping a photo on their phone sounded behind me.

I needed to get out of there, but Wyatt was my ride. And he was gone.

Gone. He's gone.

I replayed the last few minutes in my mind like a movie. Me telling Wyatt nothing good had come from us... his bewilderment at realizing I'd lied to him... the hurt in his eyes when I'd called him a mistake.

Oh God. Holy mother of all things... What have I done?

Rachel came out the front door just as I was rushing back inside. She grabbed my arms to stop me. "We need to go."

"No," I protested. "I need to fix this."

"Not now," she said quietly. "People are watching. Besides that, Wyatt is so pissed, he can't see straight. Now is not the time."

I allowed her to lead me to her car. Numbly, I got in, and she drove in the direction of our apartment. During the five-minute ride, my phone buzzed incessantly with notifications of me being tagged on social media. I couldn't stop myself from looking at them. Most were innocent.

Ohmigod! I sat next to Katelyn Sterling in class for an entire semester and didn't realize it!

Katelyn Sterling and Wyatt Archer are dating! Holy shit!

But some were less than kind.

Katelyn Sterling—can I get a vag pic so I can complete my set?

It was everything I'd feared, only much worse because I'd also lost Wyatt. And that was one hundred percent my fault.

Rachel parked, and I dragged myself up the stairs and went straight to my room. My phone continued to buzz incessantly, but my hands shook so badly that I couldn't seem to turn it off. I threw it against the wall, and when that still didn't stop it, I slammed it on the edge of my dresser again and again.

Hugging the stuffed blue unicorn to my chest, I collapsed on my bed. I didn't come out the rest of the night.

* * *

I BARELY SLEPT. My time with Wyatt played through my mind, from our awkward beginning to me screaming at him outside of Los Ranchos, and everything in between. And there was so much in between: Wyatt tucking me in his coat at Snow Scene, watching me intently at the gym, loving me with his body. But I would never forget the disdainful look that had been in his eyes last night.

What have I done?

Was my anonymity worth hurting Wyatt? Was it worth giving him up? I'd thought staying under the radar was the most important thing, but now I was more concerned about losing Wyatt than having my picture taken at the grocery store. How could I have been so stupid? Being with Wyatt had changed my life—changed me—but I hadn't updated my priorities. Instead, I had been stuck worrying about my past, when in the end, it wasn't my past that had screwed me over. No, I'd done that myself.

Rachel lightly knocked on my door.

"Come in," I called softly.

She opened the door. Princess Buttercup was in her arms. *Huh.* I hadn't realized the feline wasn't in my room like usual. I must have been in a bad way if even the princess gave me a wide berth.

"Hey," Rachel said. "Your dad called my phone to ask about you. He said you aren't answering yours, and he was worried."

I looked away guiltily. "I broke it." It had been such a childish thing to do. I couldn't help but recall my and Wyatt's conversation about money. If I didn't have a healthy bank account, would I have been so blasé with such an expensive item? I liked to think that I'd separated myself from Katelyn Sterling, but the more I thought about it, the more I realized that wasn't possible. My past had made me money, but it had also shaped me into the person I was today. How many decisions had I made based purely on my Katelyn Sterling experience? I could think of at least one very bad, very big one.

How could I have told Wyatt that being with him was a mistake? I couldn't answer that question, and I was no closer to justifying my actions. I had been upset and hurting, and I'd lashed out. If he'd known what was going on, I had no doubt he would have tried to shield me from those stupid girls at the restaurant. But I hadn't given him the chance. I hadn't trusted him enough, and that had been my biggest mistake.

Rachel didn't comment on the broken phone. "I told him you were fine, but I wanted to check and make sure I wasn't lying."

My eyes filled with tears, and I was surprised there were any left. "I'm not fine."

"Oh, honey." Rachel came to sit beside me on the bed. She released Princess Buttercup and wrapped her arms around me. "The night is darkest before the dawn."

Through my tears, I couldn't help but let out a small laugh. "Song lyrics? Really?"

She shrugged. "I'm pretty sure that was a saying before people put it into songs." She raised an eyebrow. "This too shall pass?" Her attempt at humor fell flat.

"I don't think it will."

For starters, my secret was out. That would change almost everything in my life. Or maybe not. Maybe people wouldn't care about a has-been like me after the initial hubbub died down. I didn't know, but I guessed I was about to find out. It just didn't seem as catastrophic as it once had. In a way, I felt freer because I didn't have to hide anymore. I hadn't realized how much the secret had weighed on me.

Rachel picked at a mat in Princess Buttercup's hair. "I'd like to say you're overreacting, but I have no personal experience with this."

Guilt slammed into me. I'd been so wrapped up in my own misery, I hadn't considered that Wyatt wasn't the only one I'd lied to. Rachel had every right to be pissed at me and feel betrayed, yet she was comforting me.

"Are you mad?" I asked her quietly. "That I lied to you?"

"I figured you'd tell me when you were ready."

I frowned. "Wait, what?"

She looked at me like I had a third eye in the middle of my forehead. "Did you think I didn't know?"

"Yes. I…" I didn't know what to say.

Rachel rolled her eyes. "I've lived with you for the past three years. I'm just going to pretend that you don't actually think I'm stupid enough to have been fooled this whole time."

"I don't think you're stupid," I protested. "I just thought that I—"

"What? That you were a better secret keeper?" Rachel snorted. "You would never make it as a spy. Why do you think the Double Ds call you Hollywood?"

I was flabbergasted. "They know too?"

"Well, yeah." She said it in a *well, duh* tone. "They practically live with us. Danielle was obsessed with *Sisters Squared* when she was younger. She had the bedsheets and everything."

"No, she didn't." I was mortified by the thought of my friend sleeping on a life-size image of Kassidy and me.

Rachel nodded solemnly. "She totally did. She probably still has them. Besides that, you're way too good at charades to not have acting experience."

"Charades isn't acting!"

"Isn't it, though?" She held up her thumb and forefinger an inch apart. "Just a little bit?"

"Maybe," I allowed. I was dumbfounded by the fact that the girls had known my truth the whole time but had never let on. They'd let me continue my ruse. I felt like a moron. "Why didn't you call me on it?"

She shrugged. "Like I said, I figured you'd tell me when you were ready. I just didn't think it would take this long."

It shouldn't have taken me so long, and it shouldn't have come out like it had. I loved Rachel like a sister. Hell, some days I loved her more than my real sister. What was the point of getting close to people if I was going to hold such an important part of me back?

I'd been such an idiot. It was amazing how clearly I saw everything now that I'd royally screwed it all up.

"I need to talk to Wyatt." I wasn't going to make the same mistake twice and insulate myself while I worked through my feelings.

"You can use my phone," Rachel offered.

That's right. My phone was broken.

I shook my head. "Thanks, but this is a conversation we need to have in person."

* * *

Wyatt

I'D SPENT THE previous night scouring the internet for every scrap of information I could find about Katie Sul—*Christ.* Katelyn Sterling.

I couldn't believe I hadn't even known her goddamn name. To be fair, Sullivan was probably her legal name while Sterling was a stage name, but still. The point remained the same.

Katie and her sister had been a national sensation when they were kids. Some people compared them to Mary-Kate and Ashley Olsen. Many of those same people said the Sterling sisters had easily surpassed the Olsens' level of fame. Between the TV show, a few movies, and merchandise, they'd made millions. Their faces had been everywhere, and little girls had idolized them. There were a few frightening articles about a man who'd broken into their hotel room and waited for them. Nothing happened, but that was some scary shit. They'd been ten at the time.

Fuck. Once I'd started reading, it had been a rabbit hole I couldn't climb out of. Next came all the recent scandals about her sister, Kassidy. I hadn't even known she had a damn sister. Then there were the mentions of Mama Sterling, who sounded like a nightmare.

But I didn't understand why she hadn't told me all of this. Did she think I would hold it against her? The question ran through my mind all night, and by the morning, I still didn't have an answer.

I should have been waking up with her beside me in my bed. Instead, I was up at six, having gotten little sleep. The trouble was I couldn't fall back asleep, and I wasn't in the mood to do anything, even work out. There had never been a time I wasn't in the mood to work out, even when I was a kid. Not only was it a way to relieve stress, but it was my time to think. Yet I wasn't sure I wanted to be alone with my thoughts. But fuck, I sure as hell didn't want company either. Freddie had kept calling last night until I'd finally turned my phone off. I hoped he would get the hint and let me be for a while. I didn't want to do something I would have to apologize for later.

Now I wondered if Katie had been right, if it would have been cleaner to end things earlier. She'd said she had seen this coming. I hadn't because I'd been totally in the dark. Although now that I knew, so much stuff made sense, like her aversion to my slight fame, how she understood the pressures I was under, and why she rarely talked about her family. Looking at pictures of her then and now, I didn't know how she'd managed to fly under the radar for so long. Of course, no one expected a child star to be hiding as a college student in rural Virginia.

I flipped through the channels, trying to find something to distract me, but my thoughts were too loud. *Fuck it.* I didn't feel like working out, but I was going to anyway. There had never been a time when I regretted going for a run.

I changed my clothes and searched for a pair of earbuds. I didn't usually listen to music, but I thought it might help. Hell, I would try almost anything at that point. I slammed the door behind me and trotted out to the parking lot.

And I nearly ran directly into Katie.

I stared at her. She looked like hell. Her eyes were puffy, and her face was splotchy. She'd been crying. My anger toward her softened a bit before I came back to my senses. She wasn't the victim—*she'd* lied to *me*.

She shoved her hands in the pockets of her hoodie. "Are you going for a run?" Her voice sounded small, and my instinct was to pull her to my chest and tell her everything would be okay. But it wasn't. Her words echoed in my mind. *Being with you was a mistake.*

The thing was that I had loved being with Katie. She brought out the best in me. Too bad the reverse wasn't true.

"Yeah." I turned on my heel to go the other direction. Small talk with Katie was the last thing I wanted.

"Wyatt, wait. Please."

Turning slowly, I stayed silent because I had nothing to say.

"I'm sorry," she said in a rush. "I'm so sorry for the hateful things I said. I never meant to hurt you."

"You didn't," I said coldly. *A lie.* She'd dug into my chest and ripped my heart into a million pieces. She hadn't hurt me—she'd destroyed me.

She paused. That obviously wasn't what she'd expected me to say. "None of this is your fault."

"Some of it is," I corrected. "You were right—I should have let you go."

My words hit their mark, and she flinched. "I want to make things right between us. How do I do that?"

"You can't." I wished she could, but her deception wasn't something she could undo.

Taking a deep breath, she stepped toward me. When she reached her hand up, I backed away, and her arm fell listlessly at her side. "There has to be a way to fix this."

"You lied to me." My voice was low and came out more menacing than I'd intended.

"I know. I'm sorry about that. It's just that I separated myself from Katelyn Sterling. I'm not that girl anyway. It's not who I am." She added that last part quietly, like she was trying to convince herself of that fact.

"I obviously don't know who you are." I didn't even know if the girl I'd fallen in love with was real or just a façade. The deceit left a bitter aftertaste.

"Yes, you do. I'm the same person I've been this whole time." She bit her lip and blinked to clear the tears from her eyelashes. "I know you care about me. We're worth saving. Because, Wyatt, I... I love you."

The ice coating my heart thawed at those three little words. I'd been wanting to hear them on her lips more than anything, but now I couldn't take them at face value. If she could lie about something as massive as her identity, then what else could she lie about? *Everything.*

I couldn't trust her. But more than that, it hurt that she hadn't trusted me. It was only now that she was forced to be honest that she was willing to admit the truth. I wondered how long she would have kept up the ruse otherwise.

I moved farther away from her. "I don't trust you. I can't. And you've shown that you don't trust me."

"I do—"

"Don't." I fought to keep my voice steady. "I don't want to do this with you. It's done. We're done." I turned to start my run then turned back one last time. "Do you still have my key?"

She nodded.

"Get your stuff out of my place while I'm gone. Leave the key on the counter."

Then I ran away—from her, from the pain, from all of it.

CHAPTER 22

Katie

I WATCHED HIM until he turned the corner and I couldn't see him anymore. If I thought it would have made a difference, I would have run after him. But it wasn't like I would actually be able to catch him. So I did what he asked—I went into his apartment for the last time and gathered the few things I'd left there. In his bedroom, I paused, so tempted to take one of his T-shirts that I often slept in so at least I would have his scent with me for a few more days.

Pathetic.

I'd done this, and now I had to woman up and bear the consequences.

I can't believe it's over.

With one final look at his apartment, I laid the key on the counter and left. I managed to make it back to my place before I broke.

Though Rachel tried to console me, there was nothing she could say that would make it better. Hell, there was nothing *I* could say that would make it better. Though my conversation with Wyatt had been brief, his hard expression and the cold look in his eyes told me all I needed to know. His indifference was what hurt worst of all. I told myself that I would hurt less if he were hurting more, but I wasn't sure if that were actually true.

On Monday morning, I turned off my alarm clock without getting out of bed. I thought the routine of going to class would help, but I wasn't ready to face the world. My pain over losing Wyatt was bad enough, but I also had to deal with my identity as Katelyn Sterling being public knowledge. Though, to be honest, I hadn't given that much thought. I still wasn't wild about it, but compared to losing Wyatt, it simply wasn't important.

Much to Princess Buttercup's delight, I stayed in bed all day. She fluffed the pillow beside me, and I didn't even care that she was digging her claws into my high-thread-count sheets.

On Tuesday morning, Rachel barged in and opened my blinds. The light shone directly in my face, so I shoved my head under the pillow.

"You need to get up," she said.

"Cut me some slack. I—"

"No." She stripped the blankets off my body. "I cut you slack yesterday and Sunday, but today you need to get up. You might not care much about your classes right now, but I guarantee in two weeks, you will regret blowing them off."

"It doesn't matter," I grumbled. "Let's say I go to med school and become a doctor. Can you imagine walking into the exam room and finding Katelyn Sterling from *Sisters Squared* waiting to take your blood pressure?"

Rachel put her hands on her hips. "There are so many things wrong with that question. To start, you don't go by Katelyn Sterling anymore. Katelyn Sullivan is your legal name. And by the time you're a doctor, do you think anyone will still care about *Sisters Squared*? But the last and most troubling thing is that doctors don't take blood pressure. They have nurses for that. So the fact that you don't know that makes me question your capacity for becoming a doctor in the first place."

I shot her a dirty look. "I do know that. It was a hypothetical situation."

"Get your hypothetical ass out of bed. It is my duty as your BFF to give you the tough love you need right now."

She could take her BFF duties and shove them.

"Fine. I'm going." I didn't move.

She yanked the pillow away from me and threw it across the room. *Damn it!* Now I would have to risk my physical well-being to try to steal Princess Buttercup's pillow or get up to retrieve mine.

"Now!" Rachel barked. "I have to leave, but I'm not going until you're up. You're going to make me late."

I hauled my ass out of bed and went to the bathroom. After using the toilet, I turned on the shower. As soon as I heard the front door open and close, I shut off the water and ambled back to bed, scooping up my lost pillow on the way. Rachel was probably right, but I still wasn't ready.

Just one more day. I could barely stand to think about Wyatt, much less process our split. Breaking up with an average person would have been hard enough, but Wyatt wasn't average—he was famous. I was bound to see his picture somewhere on campus.

Also, people had taken pictures at Los Ranchos. Hell, our fight could have even been filmed for all I knew. The footage could be circulating on social media along with the article that identified me. Probably the only smart thing I'd done since Saturday was stay off social media, which hadn't been too hard considering my phone was broken anyway. Still, I couldn't bear to face my classmates, wondering if they'd seen everything about me online. If even one of them expressed concern or asked a well-intentioned question, I wouldn't be able to hold my shit together. That would just add fodder to the fire, and I would be forced to flee campus. So what was the point in going at all?

No, I was better off lying low for now. Having fully convinced myself, I pulled on an eye mask and went back to sleep.

A pounding on the front door woke me from my midmorning nap. Princess Buttercup arched her back and hissed at me, like it was my fault her slumber had been disturbed.

"What about my slumber?" I asked. "Did you ever consider that?"

I had no idea who it was, but I was in no shape to see anyone. It was probably just a door-to-door salesman. Who else would it be at 10:48 in the morning?

The pounding started again. *Holy crap.* It sounded like a hammer, or at least someone with big-ass hands.

I sat up so quickly, I jerked my neck. *Wyatt had big-ass football-player hands—it could be him.* Impossible hope blossomed in my chest. I jumped out of bed and nearly tripped because of the sheet that was tangled around my ankles. I raced to the door and flung it open.

It wasn't Wyatt. But I couldn't have been more shocked at who it was.

Kassidy.

She was thinner than she'd been the last time I saw her. We both had naturally slender builds, but she appeared almost skeletal. I hadn't noticed it in the recent pictures of her and Tate, but as the saying went, the camera added ten pounds. Plus, my attention had been diverted elsewhere.

"Surprise!" My sister pulled me into a hug, and it felt like I was being embraced by toothpicks. I felt the immediate need to feed her.

"What are you doing here?" I asked when she released me.

Her smile faltered just a smidge. "Aren't you happy to see me?"

"Of course." I pulled her in for another hug, both to reassure her and give me a moment to get my emotions in check. "Come in," I said as I released her.

She pulled a ridiculously huge suitcase over the threshold, parked it just inside the door, and lowered the handle. Putting her hands on her hips, she looked around.

What must she think of my small apartment? I could have afforded something much bigger and more luxurious, but even if the little college town had more opulent options, I wouldn't have wanted that. Rachel wouldn't have been able to afford her half, and I wasn't comfortable in those surroundings anymore anyway.

"What are you doing here?" I asked again. Only this time, I kept my tone upbeat and a smile on my face.

"I caught a red-eye," she said.

"Yes, but why?"

"We haven't seen each other in forever, and I figured since the secret was out, there was nothing stopping me from coming for a visit." She gave me a smug look. "You should have told me you were dating the Archer. Even I know who he is."

That was all it took for me to burst into tears, and even through my crying, I felt vindicated by my earlier justification for not going to class. I told Kassidy the whole messy story.

"He's a complete and utter moron," she said when I'd finished. "That's the only explanation why he wouldn't be with you right now."

I shook my head. "No, Kass. He's not. He's really not." I sniffed. "He's just about perfect." Perfect for me, anyway, and I'd screwed it up. The only reason I wasn't with him was staring at me in the mirror.

Kassidy pursed her lips. "Have you learned nothing from me? Don't go falling in love with someone who isn't in love with you first. You lose all the power that way."

"It's not about power." I frowned. "You can't help who you fall in love with."

She snorted. "Oh, yes, you can."

Maybe in Hollywood.

Kassidy didn't live in the real world. On her plane of existence, spreading lewd photographs of herself all over the internet was a way to get ahead. So it didn't surprise me that she didn't understand.

My sister wrinkled her nose. "Don't take this the wrong way, but when is the last time you showered?"

I instinctively leaned down to catch a whiff of my pit. It wasn't the best, but she shouldn't have been able to smell me. "Uh... Saturday?"

"That's what I thought. Shower and get dressed. We're going out."

"It's not even noon. Where exactly do you think we're going to go?"

She shrugged. "Hell if I know. What is there to do in this Podunk town?"

* * *

I MANAGED TO persuade Kassidy to hang out at my apartment for the day with a promise of going out that night. But she was antsy, and I worried she would go out without me, so I waited until Rachel was home to shower.

Having Kassidy in my apartment was surreal—something I never thought would happen. Two very separate worlds in my life had collided. I never thought I would say this, but it was actually kind of nice. The hours I'd spent with Kassidy that afternoon made me realize how much I'd missed her and how unfair it was to the both of us for me to cut her out of my life except for the occasional phone call. *That changes today.*

When I got out of the shower, laughter came from the living room. I peeked around the corner to see Rachel,

Destiny, and Danielle sitting around Kassidy, who had apparently been telling some sort of story. I'd forgotten how dazzling Kassidy could be when she was "on," and she was definitely on. She was totally in her element as the center of attention.

"Is Jackson Winthrop really a bad kisser?" Destiny asked. Jackson had played Kassidy's love interest on *Cali Girls* in the first season, and he'd gone on to star in another show. Recently, a few of his costars and former leading ladies had called out his kissing technique, saying that kissing him was like having a wet vacuum attached to their mouths.

"Ladies never kiss and tell," Kassidy said slyly, then she grinned. "Good thing for you I'm not a lady."

"So he *is* a bad kisser!" Destiny said. "I knew there was a reason all those scenes are shot from a distance."

I ducked back down the hall to go to my room and get dressed. Before I shut my door, I heard Kassidy ask, "What's the deal with this Wyatt guy?"

There was a pause, and I imagined Rachel was trying to figure out what to say. She wouldn't want to betray my confidence.

It was Danielle who spoke first. "Honestly, he's a great guy. From what I can tell anyway. I don't know him well."

Destiny snorted. "You're forgetting about how he used to go through girls like most people go through trash bags." *Good old Destiny.* When it came to guys and her friends, she was one hundred percent on her friends' sides, even if her friends were in the wrong.

"But he didn't do that with her," Danielle protested. "Everybody makes mistakes. People change." And that was Danielle in a nutshell—her big heart always saw the best in people.

"You know Katie—she's always been a little uptight," Rachel said. I made a face at that comment. While it was true, I didn't like that "uptight" was a commonly known trait of mine. "But she was a lot freer with him. He was good for her. He made her happy."

"Until he didn't," Kassidy said with venom in her tone.

"Until he didn't," Rachel confirmed. "But it's complicated."

"It's not for me," Kassidy retorted. "He made my sister cry. If I get a chance to make him pay for that, I will."

Her threat reminded me of Freddie offering to beat up Adam for Rachel. The only difference was that Kassidy wasn't joking.

CHAPTER 23

Katie

I FOUND MYSELF nervous as we headed out for the evening. Kassidy was used to the glitz and glamour of Hollywood. What would she think of the somewhat dingy college bars we were taking her to? I tried to gauge her reaction as we drove down Main Street, but she didn't give anything away as she peered out the window.

Luckily, since it was Tuesday, we easily found parking. Hopefully that meant the bars wouldn't be crowded. I still wasn't in the mood to be with the masses, even though spending time with Kassidy had actually brought me out of my funk a little. I'd forgotten how calming it could be to be in her presence. It didn't make sense because Kassidy was all drama, all the time. I chalked it up to a twin thing.

My sister strutted down the sidewalk, turning heads. Even if she weren't famous, she would still demand attention—she had an aura about her that worked like a magnet and drew people to her. My friends were evidence of that. They'd taken to her right away, so much so that I felt like I was the fifth wheel in the group. The four of them charged ahead, ready to have a fun night, while I straggled behind.

I didn't want to be out. I wanted to be tucked away in my room, studying and exchanging the occasional text with Wyatt as had become my habit on weeknights. But neither of those things were happening this evening.

At the first bar, Kassidy plunked down her credit card. "Tonight is on me." My sister obviously didn't have the same misgivings I did about flashing money around. Though it wasn't something we talked about, I imagined she had a lot more of it than I did.

She ordered a round of shooters for all of us. She held hers up in a toast. "To new friends"—she looked at Rachel, Danielle, and Destiny, who grinned—"and new beginnings." She shot me a pointed look for that last part.

As we threw back the bright-red liquid, I was all too aware of the camera phones pointing at us. I'd been afraid of this. But by the time we were on our third shooter in ten minutes, I realized that I wasn't garnering all that much attention. Perhaps if it had just been me out, people would've been more interested in taking pictures of Katelyn Sterling. But Kassidy Sterling was way more famous, so her presence took the heat off me. I hadn't expected that. My buzzed brain tried to figure out how I felt about it, and I ultimately determined that it wasn't important. That night, I was going to blow off steam—years of it, from my first stressful days of trying to live a normal life as a teen to making the ultimate mistake and losing Wyatt. My feelings could wait until tomorrow. In fact, they could wait until tomorrow's tomorrow. I was done with feelings because I was done hurting.

Kassidy quickly grew bored. "What else does this town have to offer?"

The Basement probably hadn't been the best place to bring my sister, considering its idea of quality entertainment was a few dart boards, but it was the first bar we'd come to. The next place was much more populated, and Kassidy preened at the attention she was getting. It made me realize that in Hollywood, Kassidy was probably considered a small-potatoes celebrity, nowhere near as big as Jennifer Lawrence or Scarlett Johansson. But there in Bleaksburg, Kassidy was hot shit.

I couldn't help but compare her fame to how Wyatt had described his, essentially a big fish in a little pond. I wondered...

Nope. Don't think about him. No feelings tonight, remember? More shots would help with that.

By the time the girls decided they wanted to dance, I was good and wasted. Kassidy had had as much to drink as me, but she wasn't wobbling on her feet like I was. Her tolerance was much higher, another way we were no longer identical. It made me sad.

Hell. More feelings. I would have to have another shot.

We went to Preston's next. It usually catered to the hipster crowd, but on Tuesday nights, they brought in a DJ, and it turned into the hottest club in Bleaksburg, which was to say it was the only club. Still, as I twirled on the dance floor with my friends, I couldn't help but think the disco ball and strobe lights were a nice touch. Brilliant, really.

Kassidy sat at the bar, surrounded by VVU's most eligible bachelors. Some of them probably weren't even eligible, but whatever. If they wanted to act a fool because a celebrity was in their midst, that was on them. They could take it up with their girlfriends later.

Rachel yelled in my ear to be heard above the music. "I think college life agrees with your sister."

I snorted. *Partying* agreed with my sister. I doubted she would take to attending classes and studying, which was the most important aspect of college life, at least for me. When we'd been tutored on the set of *Sisters Squared*, Kassidy would do everything to get out of it. It was a small miracle she had managed to get a high school diploma.

Kassidy waved me and the girls over to the bar, where she had another round of shooters waiting. "These are courtesy of Trent." She beamed at the guy standing next to her.

"Brent," he corrected, but he didn't seem too bothered by the mistake.

She waved her hand dismissively. "That's what I said." She held her hand up to her mouth and whispered to me, "That's not what I said." She rolled her eyes.

After we downed the shooters, there was another guy waiting in line to buy us another round. Apparently, Kassidy had made it clear that she only accepted drinks if they were bought for all of us. While I appreciated her loyalty and quickness to include my friends as part of her entourage, she wasn't doing us any favors. None of us could keep up with her, but of course in our inebriated states, none of us would admit it. In fact, the more I drank, the better the idea of going out seemed. I couldn't remember why I had been opposed to it in the first place. Every ounce I ingested pushed away my feelings. The incredible pain that had taken up residence in my heart the last few days was muted to a dull ache. *Manageable.*

In short order, I found myself sitting next to Kassidy, basking in the glow of attention. I was adored. I was *loved.* There was no pressure to do anything but exist and pose for pictures. No wonder my sister relished it.

A nagging errant thought in my mind kept telling me that the attention was superficial, that these people didn't really care about me. They didn't even know me, and I sure as hell didn't know them.

I pushed the thought away. I'd been rejected by the one person I'd tried to give my heart to, so there was no harm in accepting a little love from strangers. I needed it. I needed to feel important, if only for a moment. I needed to feel like I mattered.

Kassidy and I danced, and though her moves were much better—and sexier—than mine, I didn't care. People loved us. People loved *me*. It was just perfect.

Then Rachel had to go and ruin it by trying to pull me off the dance floor. I wrestled my arm out of her grasp. "I'm not done!"

"Honey, we should go," she said.

"No," I said firmly, taking the shot that Kassidy held out. We'd graduated from shooters to straight liquor. And I wasn't one of those drunks who was unsteady on her feet. *No sirree.* With every drink, my dance moves became even more on point. *I am a dancing goddess.*

My sister shimmied, and I shook. Somehow our actions morphed into a dance sequence that we'd filmed for the series finale of *Sisters Squared.* I hadn't realized I still remembered the stupid choreography that had taken forever to learn. When we finished, we threw our arms around each other and laughed. Noticing people filming us, I smiled wider. *Because hello?* We were awesome, and awesomeness deserved to be documented. Awesomeness deserved to be loved. *I* deserved to be loved.

Rachel stood on the edge of the dance floor, looking concerned. *That simply won't do.* I hadn't meant to leave my bestie on the sidelines, and it was time to remedy that.

I grasped her hand to pull her onto the floor. "Come on!"

She resisted. "I really think we should go."

"Why? Aren't you having fun?"

A wrinkle formed at the top of her nose, right between her eyes. That was her worried look. "It's late. Let's go. Please?"

I didn't want to go. I wanted to continue being adored by my adoring fans—well, they were most likely Kassidy's fans, but whatever. I wanted to keep being adored and having that adoration fill the holes in my heart. There were so many. Wyatt had done a number on— *Oops! I broke my own rule. No thinking about him.*

I held up five fingers. "Five more minutes."

Rachel nodded. "Okay."

I spun to return to dancing, and my eyes landed on someone across the room. Multiple someones, actually. Freddie and Angela. They were looking at me, but it wasn't with adoring expressions. They looked worried. No, that wasn't it. It was worse—pity.

Oh my God. All the muted feelings returned at full volume, and it was like getting hit by a semi. I hurt everywhere—my heart, my head, my lungs. I couldn't breathe. I stumbled and would have fallen if Kassidy hadn't caught me.

"Are you okay?" she asked.

My eyes locked with Freddie's. "I need to get out of here." None of this was real—it was all superficial and stupid. This wasn't my life. This wasn't *me.*

Kassidy peered at me. "Katie, what's wrong?"

"Wyatt's best friend is here. I can't face him right now. Oh God. What if Wyatt is here? I can't see him."

Kassidy pursed her lips, and I could tell she wanted to stay. She probably hoped Wyatt would show so she could give him a piece of her mind.

I looked over to where Freddie had been standing, but he wasn't there. Scanning the crowd, I easily located his tall body towering over everyone. He was weaving his way through the masses to reach me. *Shit.*

"I'm leaving." I disentangled myself from Kassidy and bolted for the front door, knocking into a few people in my haste to get out. Leaning against the brick wall outside the bar, I sucked in air, suddenly feeling sick to my stomach. I put my face in my hands as everything overwhelmed me— losing Wyatt, how I'd acted all evening, and what my new reality would be like. Sure, I'd welcomed the attention tonight, but it wasn't something that could be turned on and off. I'd set a scary precedent.

To my left, I heard the click of a camera, and not just the small electronic click of a camera phone. I turned. A man had a huge camera pointed at me. This thing looked like it belonged on a safari in the Sahara. The lens was almost as long as my arm. The man behind the camera clicked away.

"No pictures, please," I said as politely as I could muster. I was out of practice, but this was my new reality, so I'd better relearn the skill quick.

He ignored me. "Where's your sister?"

Shit. I had been waiting for her and my friends to come outside, but now I needed to get away from this guy. I looked around, trying to figure out how to lose him. Unfortunately, Kassidy appeared.

"Hell yeah." The man snapped away. "Kassidy, look over here, sweetheart."

She ignored him. "Are you okay?" she asked me.

I wasn't, but I nodded. "Let's just get out of here."

"Over here, ladies!"

Click, click, click.

She linked her arm through mine, and we walked down the sidewalk, away from the paparazzi. *Another day in the life of Kassidy Sterling.* I took a deep breath. The man would get what he wanted, and he'd go on his merry way.

He followed us. "Give me some good ones, girls. I'm just trying to earn a living."

We picked up the pace. Too bad we had to stop at a red light and wait to cross the street. *Click, click, click.* I ducked my chin and turned my face away, but he circled us to get a better angle. Unless we wanted to dash across traffic, there was no escape.

"That's enough," Kassidy said firmly. "I'm sure you've gotten some good shots."

"Not good enough." *Click, click, click.* His mouth stretched into a slimy smile. "But I could retire if I got a shot of your twin cunts. That baby would sell for millions. How about it?"

I recoiled at his vulgar language. *Why is this fucking light taking so long to change?*

"Enough!" Kassidy yelled. "You're filth. Paparazzi filth."

"Like I said, I'm just trying to make a living." *Click, click, click.* "And it's not like you haven't flashed your cunt before. At least do it for a good cause this time."

"Fuck you," Kassidy snarled.

His expression turned menacing. "If you're not going to play nice, then neither am I." With his camera still pointed at us, he lunged.

Kassidy shoved me behind her, and my foot slipped off the curb.

My sister shrieked my name. Then everything went dark.

CHAPTER 24

Wyatt

I NEARLY MOWED down the unfortunate nurse who happened to cross my path. Freddie's words played on repeat in my mind. *"Blood everywhere, so much blood. They took her in an ambulance."*

I hadn't needed to hear more than that. I'd run out the door so fast, I'd forgotten to put on a shirt. Luckily, I'd had one in the back seat of my car. But honestly, I didn't give a shit. I would've liked to see them try to kick me out of the hospital for improper attire or some bullshit. Nothing could keep me from Katie.

Fuck. I'd been so cold and heartless to her the last time I'd seen her. And now she was in the goddamn emergency room. Freddie couldn't tell me anything else besides the fact that there had been cops, lots of blood, and an ambulance.

Trying to figure out who would tell me where she was, I looked wildly around the emergency room. I spotted a check-in desk and strode over to it. *God help this woman if she tries to pull any of the family-only shit.* But before I could ask her about Katie, someone came up behind me.

"What the hell are you doing here?" The voice was laced with hatred, but that wasn't what caught my attention. It had a hint of familiarity about it.

I turned. *Holy shit.* Kassidy *fucking* Sterling. My immediate thought was that she and Katie looked nothing alike. Sure, there was a resemblance, but I never would have pegged them as identical twins. Katie was naturally beautiful, while Kassidy looked overly done up. Fake.

Though she apparently wasn't happy to see me there, I was glad to see her. She could save me from dealing with hospital bureaucracy bullshit.

"Where is she?" I asked.

Kassidy planted her hands on her hips. "Oh, so now you care."

I ground my teeth. "Just tell me where she is."

Lifting her nose in the air, she evaluated me coolly. I was about to give up on getting the info from her and try the nurse instead when she spoke.

"She's in surgery."

Surgery... The one little word made me stumble backward. Collapsing into a chair, I put my head in my hands.

Blood everywhere, so much blood.

Oh God. The image of Katie covered in blood and being sliced open on an operating table flashed in my mind.

"How bad is it?" I choked out the words.

Kassidy let out a sob, causing me to look up at her. Tears flowed down her cheeks, leaving streaks in her makeup. "The doctor hasn't come to talk to me."

Oh shit, oh fuck, oh no, no, no. It was bad.

"She'll be okay," I told her, as if my will could make it so. "She'll be okay. She has to be." I couldn't accept any other outcome. "Tell me what happened."

Kassidy sank into the chair next to me. "There was an accident. She..." Her crying thickened, and she turned away, unable to speak.

I ran my hands over my head. I'd been such an idiot. I'd been so damn self-righteous. Yeah, she'd lied to me, big time. But if I'd been in her position, what would I have done? We'd only been together a few months, and she'd kept her secret for years. Maybe I had expected too much from her too soon. Besides that, the fact that she'd been a child star had no bearing whatsoever on our relationship. Except when I'd refused to accept her apology.

I was such an asshole. And now Katie was hurt, bad enough to need surgery and bad enough that her sister had come all the way from California.

Wait... how did she get here so fast?

Not important. All that mattered was Katie getting better so I could tell her what an asshole I'd been and beg for forgiveness. And maybe, just maybe she would let me make it up to her. I couldn't believe how I'd treated her. She'd told me she loved me, and I had blown her off. And for what? I couldn't think of any reason good enough. Now there I was, hoping she would treat me better than I'd treated her.

I loved this girl with everything I had, and I'd let my foolish pride get in the way of that. *Never again.*

"Kassidy, I'm ready to..." I looked up, and there she was—Katie. I couldn't speak.

Her hand went to her throat, and she swallowed thickly. "What are you doing here?"

I stood, still not believing what I was seeing. I'd just been imagining the worst, and now she was standing there, whole and healthy. Well, not completely. She had a huge knot on her forehead and a bandage wrapped around her hand. Even so, she'd never looked more beautiful in my eyes.

Beside me, Kassidy also stood. She cleared her throat and wiped her eyes. "Are you cleared to leave?"

What... in... the... fuck? A second ago, she was crying like her sister was dying, and now she was totally unruffled. If not for the streaks in her makeup, I would have sworn I'd imagined the whole thing.

"Freddie told me an ambulance took you," I said slowly. "And that there was a lot of blood." I turned to Kassidy. "You said she was in surgery!"

She shrugged. "Getting stitches is minor surgery, right?"

I couldn't even find it in myself to be pissed, not when Katie was right in front of me.

I closed the distance between us and took her in my arms.

* * *

Katie

WYATT'S ARMS WERE around me, holding me so tight, I could feel his racing heart. Closing my eyes, I enjoyed something I'd thought I would never experience again—the feeling of his body against mine. I inhaled his scent, and with it, intimate memories filled my mind. I struggled to keep my composure.

As he held me, his breathing slowly steadied. When he released me, disappointment filled the void he'd left. Kassidy was nowhere in sight.

"I thought..." He trailed off. "I don't know what I thought. Freddie called. He said something about blood and an ambulance, and then when I got here, Kassidy was sobbing about an accident."

I bit my lip to keep it from trembling. "All of those things are true. Sort of. There was blood, an ambulance, and an accident." Freddie had obviously seen the aftermath, and in true Freddie form, he must have embellished the details.

I told Wyatt about the aggressive paparazzi and how he'd threatened us. The last thing I remembered was slipping off the curb. When I woke in the ambulance, I was covered in blood, and my hand and head hurt like hell. Apparently, I'd hit my head on the curb when I'd landed, and my hand had somehow gotten cut on a broken bottle that was in the gutter. My falling into the street had resulted in a fender bender as a driver swerved to avoid me. The paparazzi had taken off by that point, and he was wanted for questioning.

Now with the emergency room and Wyatt, it had been one hell of a night.

Wyatt pulled me to him again and kissed the aching lump on my forehead. My breath caught. He was being so tender with me—such a tease of things I couldn't have. But it was nice to know he still cared about me on some level. Maybe we could get to the point of being friends. Except I wasn't sure I could ever manage that. Being around him made me yearn for more, and I didn't see that changing.

"It's my fault," Wyatt said softly. "I'm so sorry. It's my fault."

Now I was confused. "What's your fault?"

"This." He placed another kiss on the lump. "And this." He kissed my bandage. "I should have been there. If I were there, that guy wouldn't have harassed you."

"He probably still would have," I said. "Paparazzi are relentless."

"Then I could have protected you."

"It's not anyone's responsibility to protect me." His words hurt my heart—he was there out of guilt. But guilt indicated he still cared. Too bad that wasn't enough for me.

"You knew," he said. "And you told me. You knew that if your secret got out, something like this could happen."

That was true. I'd counted on some embarrassing pictures of me caught midchew at a restaurant or my ass showing up in a celebrity cellulite column. I'd never imagined I would end up bloody and in the hospital within a few days of being outed.

"It goes with the territory." I laughed bitterly. "I learned that at an early age." I would never wish some of my childhood experiences on a person. Then again, I'd also had a lot of privileges. I still needed to reconcile the two truths of my past.

"I get it now. I didn't before. I understand why you kept that part of you hidden."

While I was glad he finally understood, I wished it hadn't taken an incident like this. Luckily, it wasn't my dominant hand that was injured, but it and my forehead hurt like a bitch. Plus, I still felt a little drunk, which didn't help.

I peered up at Wyatt. The gold flecks in his eyes seemed more intense than usual in the harsh hospital light. Hell, he seemed more intense than usual.

"I shouldn't have lied to you," I said. "I should have been up front about why fame freaked me out. That's the mistake I made. Being with you was never a mistake."

He shook his head. "You didn't owe me anything. I messed up. When the truth came out, I should have stuck with you to help you through it. I was too stupid to understand what it meant."

"You're not stupid."

"Oh, I'm pretty fucking stupid."

I couldn't help it—I grinned. "You're not."

"Only an idiot would let you go." He swallowed. "Especially when that idiot loves you."

Did he just say he loved me? I must still be drunk. My stomach dropped to the floor, and I put a hand on a nearby wall to steady myself. "What did you say?"

He clasped my hand and held it to his heart. "Katie, I love you. I fell so hard and so fast for you, but I never told you because I didn't want to spook you again. But fuck, Katie, I thought I'd lost you, like *really* lost you. Your sister is one hell of an actress."

"She's won awards," I said stupidly. I couldn't think. *He loves me, he loves me, he loves me.*

His blue eyes locked onto mine. "Let me make it up to you. Let me be there for you. Let me make sure nothing like this ever happens again."

I closed my eyes. "You can't." He inhaled sharply, and I rushed on. "Stuff like this is always going to be a risk, but probably not as much once people realize I'm a has-been."

"You could never be a has-been." He brought my hand to his lips and kissed each of my fingertips. "Let me rephrase my request. Let me love you, Katelyn. Just let me love you."

Exhaling, I let go of all the walls keeping my feelings at bay. When I inhaled, everything came rushing back—I felt adored, I felt like I mattered, but most importantly, I felt loved. But this time, it was real. *I'm loved.*

I captured his hand and brought his fingertips to my lips. "Only if I can love you back."

The tension in Wyatt's face slipped away as my words registered. He gently cupped my face and kissed me. It was soft, tender, and right. The harsh hospital lights and the buzz of conversations around us faded away.

"Can we go now?" The words jolted me out of the moment.

I pulled away from Wyatt to see Kassidy standing by the door, tapping her foot.

"I don't think I like your sister," Wyatt whispered in my ear.

"I heard that! And you're welcome, you dumbass. Without me, your head might still be up your ass." She narrowed her eyes at him. "But if you make my sister cry again, you'll get worse than being tricked into thinking she's dying a horrible death in surgery."

"Well, my head is thoroughly out of my ass now." Wyatt jingled his keys. "Come on. I'll drop you off at Katie's place, but she's coming home with me." He looked down at me, blasting me with a toe-curling smolder. "I need to get started on making things up to her."

I suddenly felt light-headed, and I didn't know if it was due to my head wound, the smolder, or the promise of things to come.

Definitely the smolder.

About the Author

 Jessica lives in Virginia with her college-sweetheart husband, two rambunctious sons, and two rowdy but lovable rescue dogs. Since her house is overflowing with testosterone, it's a good thing she has a healthy appreciation for Marvel movies, Nerf guns, and football.

To learn more about Jessica, visit her website jessicaruddick.com. Connect with her on Twitter at @JessicaMRuddick or on Facebook at facebook.com/AuthorJessicaRuddick.

Other Books by Jessica Ruddick

Virginia Valley University
In the Pocket
Fair Catch

The Elemental Saga
Undefined (Book One)
Untamed (Book Two)
Unleashed (Book Three)
Unveiled (Book Four)

The Legacy Series
Birthright (Book One)
Retribution (Book Two)
Sacrifice (Book Three)
Redemption (Book Four)

The Love on Campus Series
Letting Go
Wanting More

Made in United States
North Haven, CT
21 October 2021